THE DEEP END

ROBERT LIDDELL

THE DEEP END

A Novel

PETER OWEN
London & Chester Springs

A
GUIDO GRANAI

PETER OWEN PUBLISHERS
73 Kenway Road London SW5 0RE
Peter Owen books are distributed in the USA by
Dufour Editions Inc. Chester Springs PA 19425–0449

First published in 1968
Published in this edition 1993
© The Estate of Robert Liddell 1968, 1993

ISBN 0–7206–0903–8 (cased)
ISBN 0–7206–0919–4 (paper)

A catalogue record for this book is available
from the British Library

Printed and made in Great Britain by
Biddles of Guildford and King's Lynn

CHAPTER ONE

'This is a marvellous vantage-point, Aunt Mary,' said Kit Henderson, taking a seat in the bow-window of the upstairs drawing-room.

'You think it is vulgar of me to spy out of it,' said Mary Langton. 'But a headmaster's wife does like to lurk unseen on the first day of term. If I were to be seen, some mother would at once begin to bother me about her delicate little boy;. as if I knew one boy from another!'

'I wish I'd come up earlier,' said Kit. 'Then I could have got a detached view of the main batch, when they came up in the brakes from the station.'

'I call that morbid, Christopher,' said Mary. 'Will you ring for tea?'

'There's Knight greeting a parent,' said Kit. 'What do I call him, by the way?'

'"Mr Knight" to the boys of course,' said Mary. 'I think you'd better address him as "sir", as he's your uncle's junior partner; unless he tells you not to.'

'He looks as if he might want me to call him "Dudley",' said Kit uneasily. 'I couldn't do that.'

'You and I will call him "Dudley" between ourselves,' said Mary. 'That will take the edge off it for you. You could call him "you" for a bit, or only speak to him in front of the boys. There's the maid; don't let's be too obviously spying.'

'Mr Henderson and I will have tea here,' she said, as

1

the maid came in. 'Put a third cup for the headmaster, please; but we won't wait for him.'

'The maid didn't seem to disapprove of our activities,' said Kit. 'Oh, poor Peggy!' said Mary. 'She's pregnant by the knife and boot man we had last term. She told me so yesterday. That's probably rather taking up her thoughts.'

'Gracious! What will you do?'

'Let her stay on this term,' said Mary. 'It won't be obvious, and they're small boys. I wouldn't like Mr Knight to know, however.'

'"Dudley", you mean,' said Kit. 'Do you remember the "black column of a clergyman" in *Jane Eyre*? Dudley looks like a grey column of a clergyman.'

'That's because he's so modern and broadminded that he wears grey flannel,' said Mary. 'Really he looks far more clerical than he would in black.'

'A gothic column?'

'Oh, no, nothing mediaeval,' said Mary. 'I'm afraid he's a Doric column: Spartan simplicity and strength.'

'Who's the parent with him this time?'

'Lady Best-Pennant,' said Mary. 'She's not a parent; she's poor little Harry Staples' aunt. Oh, here comes tea. Thank you, Peggy. How do you like yours, Christopher?'

'A little milk please, no sugar. Dudley seems rather obsequious.'

'She lives quite near; he's been over to luncheon. He'd think she was rather grand, I daresay.'

'Is she?' asked Kit.

'Dear, no! Beastly German woman!' said Mary. 'Oh, I've shocked you, Christopher; you think I've forgotten that it's 1924, and we're generous to our defeated foes. I don't mean she's beastly just because she's a German.'

'No; beastly, and also German,' said Kit.

'And beastly in rather a Teutonic way, if you follow me?'

'Perhaps that's why Dudley's bowing in rather a continental manner over her hand,' said Kit. 'His left arm is trailing with affectionate carelessness over the boy's shoulder.'

'You're a great addition, Christopher!' said Mary fondly.

'And now there's a lovely smile full of flashing white teeth,' said Kit. 'At least one imagines it; I can't see it from here.'

'One imagines it only too well.'

'Who's that getting out of that very grand motor-car?' asked Kit.

'Little Ralph Wimbush; and there's his mother. Your Uncle Dick calls her "Charlotte the harlot"; you know how old-fashioned he is.'

'It's just like the Bible,' said Kit. 'There's a "young man of no understanding" with her.'

'How nice that you know your Old Testament,' said Mary. 'I expect that he owns the motor-car. He's probably a peer. Little Ralph will refer to him as "my uncle Barchester" or something like that; a very worldly boy.'

'Dudley's touching pitch; I hope he won't be defiled.'

'Oh, he rather likes sinners,' said Mary. 'I mean, just meeting them like this. Ah! But now there's a less agreeable meeting.'

'Why?'

'It's Colonel Gibson bringing the boy Ronald back; Dick plays golf with the Colonel, and it's rather embarrassing. The boy is such a hopelessly horrid boy.'

'In what way?'

'So utterly untrustworthy; so mean and treacherous and envious and vindictive.'

'Some of those sound very grownup faults,' said Kit.

'They begin to show themselves very early.'

3

'Poor Colonel!'

'I don't know,' said Mary. 'I daresay he isn't as nice as your uncle thinks; and, any way, he's a bad loser at golf. I expect parents get the children they deserve; not even quite as bad children as they deserve. I hate parents; never be one, Christopher.'

'I won't,' said Kit. 'Does one talk like this to Uncle Dick?'

'Yes, of course,' said Mary. 'I'd forgotten this was the first time you'd been behind the scenes, so to speak. Your uncle thinks much the same as I do. He's a bit more charitable, because he sees the better side of people. I think, in some cases, they must flash it on him, and then turn it away pretty quickly, before I catch up with them.'

They were laughing, as Richard Langton came in.

'Ring for fresh tea, Dick,' said his wife. 'This is stewed.'

'So your aunt has been amusing you, Kit?' said Dick with a smile. 'Talking wickedness about the school, I daresay.'

'I've been trying to call him "Christopher",' said Mary. 'I thought the boys might laugh at "Kit".'

'I wonder what Knight will call him,' said Dick, thoughtfully. 'Perhaps he'll get a nickname.'

'In that case it might as well be "Kit".'

'You're quite right,' said Mary. 'Now Mr Knight likes to think that the boys call him "the Dud", and that it's an affectionate nickname.'

'It is, and they do,' said Dick. 'I've heard them.'

'You know that he invented it himself?' said Mary. 'Some boys call him "Deadly Nightshade": he didn't invent that.'

'One wouldn't,' said Kit. 'But it does suit him better.'

'It gives the sinister element in him,' said Mary. 'He always makes me think of the Serpent in the Garden

4

of Eden; which isn't fair, as he is very far from subtle.'

'You know the boys are devoted to him,' said Dick reproachfully.

'Eve found the Serpent very attractive, when she was longing for the knowledge of good and evil,' said Mary.

'Do the boys want it as much as all that?' asked Kit.

'I'm afraid everyone wants it, till he's got it,' said Mary. 'And Mr Knight throws out tempting hints from time to time.'

'We take a different view of boys,' said Dick. 'Mary and I prefer to treat them as children; Knight wants to treat them as adolescents. He's always wanting to tell them things; only make them self-conscious. I put my foot down there. They've probably picked up all they need to know already, from watching animals. I just tell the leaving boys a few Bible stories on their last night— about Tamar and Onan, don't you know, and the Cities of the Plain, and so on. Then they won't be at a disadvantage when they go to their public schools.'

'Very sound,' said Kit.

'Knight is wasted here, in a way,' said Dick. 'He'd be in his element cleaning up a thoroughly immoral house at a public school. He won't realize how long the young remain innocent.'

'Here we've cut down the deadly sins to four,' said Mary. 'The boys are too young for Lust, and we give them no opportunity for Avarice or Gluttony, as we don't allow them to have private food or pocket money.'

'Envy, Anger, Pride and Sloth ought to be enough to give Dudley Knight a good game,' said Kit.

'Giant Sloth is enough for me,' said Dick. 'More than enough to fight.'

'And what about the deadly virtues?' asked Kit.

'I'm afraid they'll be introduced when your uncle retires,' said Mary.

'I must admit Knight would like to make changes,'

said Dick. 'I won't stand for them, while I'm here.'

'They're all changes in the same direction,' said Mary. 'All meant to age the poor boys. He'd begin by making us call them all by their surnames.'

'He often does it, my dear,' said Dick. 'It's caught on among some of them, I'm sorry to say.'

'We call them by their Christian names, because they're children,' said Mary. 'Fancy calling a little thing of eight "Smith-Ramsbotham"!'

'We try not to be institutional, and that's just what he doesn't like,' said Dick.

'We run the place like a private house, as much as we can,' said Mary. 'For example, if there are two different dishes served at school dinner (and sometimes this is convenient) boys are given their choice. Mr Knight can't bear that; I suppose they didn't do it at Sparta.'

'I expect there was only black broth there,' said Kit. 'Odious place!'

'The landscape is grand,' said Dick. 'Your aunt and I once took a taxi there, when we were on a Hellenic cruise. I shall never forget it.'

'Then the people had no excuse,' said Kit. 'They should have known better.'

'Our own view is not so bad,' said Mary. 'Mr Knight should know better than to want to make this place wretched with a sort of Spartan secret police.'

'Your aunt exaggerates,' said Dick. 'She means that Knight often talks about the boys taking a share in running the school. I suppose he means a sort of adaptation of the prefect system.'

'Why didn't he become a public school master?' asked Kit.

'He only took a third class degree,' said his uncle. 'He would never be allowed to teach a good form.'

'And he'd have no hope of running the place,' said Mary.

6

'Is he a disappointed man?' asked Kit.

'I don't see how he could have expected to get a better class,' said Dick. 'The man's got a third-class mind.'

'I'm never sure,' said Mary. 'Would he seem so pleased with himself if he really were? On the other hand, all that outward appearance of self-satisfaction, kept up long enough, must produce an inward feeling to correspond, don't you think?'

'Well, I suppose he has to look good, as he's a clergyman,' said Kit. 'And that gives him rather a pull over you, doesn't it?'

'We rather restrain him,' said Mary. 'Of course he reads the prayers, so the prayers are what he likes. But your uncle reads the Bible, and he reads what he likes.'

'I like the good book very much,' said Dick. 'I read it from beginning to end—leaving out genealogies, and that sort of thing. It's a book the boys ought to know: part of a gentleman's education. In four or five years here a boy hears quite a lot of it.'

'Mr Knight is always offering your uncle some new lectionary or other,' said Mary. 'He pays no attention. And I play the piano, and I just choose whatever hymn I feel in the mood for.'

'Knight tried to foist a new hymn-book on us,' said Dick. '*The Boy Scout's Hymnal Companion*, or something like that.'

'Ghastly, I should think,' said Kit.

> *'Above the belt we plant the fist,*
> *We smite the foe between the eyes;*
> *We lift red, brawny hands to Christ,*
> *Who judged the fight and gives the prize,'*

sang Mary. 'Manly, isn't it?'

'Gracious!' said Kit. 'Was that really in it?'

'You can't think I'd invent it,' said Mary. 'Of course, I

7

may have got a word or two wrong, as one does with poetry.'

'I wondered a little about the "red, brawny hands".'

'It's on adjectives that one's memory slips,' said Mary. 'I'll try to find the book for you: we were given a sample copy.'

'I hope Knight doesn't preach?' said Kit.

'He doesn't often get the chance,' said Dick. 'We take the boys to the village church on Sundays. But in bad weather, or when there's an epidemic of influenza or something...'

'You ought to be safe in the summer term, Christopher,' said his aunt.

'It's too bad of us taking up your summer like this,' said Dick. 'It was very good of you to come at such short notice and help us out. I hope you won't be the worse for interrupting your foreign languages.'

'Oh, no, Uncle Dick,' said Kit. 'I'll go abroad again directly the holidays begin; that will give me two and a half months before I have to go up to Cambridge. I couldn't have afforded to stay all the time.'

'Well, in that case, a term here may do you no harm,' said Dick rising. 'It will be long enough to warn you to do anything on earth rather than be a schoolmaster.'

'Poor Dick, he adores the school really,' said Mary, as her husband closed the door. 'He'll be lost when he retires.'

'Need he retire?' said Kit. 'I thought it was a job that could go on for ever, particularly in one's own school.'

'Dudley wants to get him out. There's a lot of talk about "Youth" these days, and I daresay parents may swallow some of it.'

'I hope they'll put up with my extreme youth for a term,' said Kit.

'Thank Heaven you are aware of it!' said Mary. 'We've had other big boys, between school and the university. I

8

remember one who was always snapping his cigarette case and flicking his lighter, to show he'd left school, and was allowed to smoke.'

'Well, that's a thing I never do,' said Kit.

'Take care you don't begin,' said Mary. 'And there was another youth who tried to grow a moustache, to see if he could.'

'And could he?'

'He could not.'

'Well, if I do, I promise I shall always wear so large a fan that it cannot be seen,' said Kit.

'And no motor-bicycles, on any account,' said Mary.

'Perish the thought!' said Kit. 'A push-bike will do for me.'

'Of course, you're a gentleman, Christopher,' said Mary. 'You will be a great comfort to your uncle and me.'

'You've said nothing about the rest of the staff,' said Kit. 'Shall I get on all right with them?'

'Well, Dudley has rather filled our horizon,' said Mary. 'I don't know why you shouldn't get on all right with the others. There's Mr MacLeod; his heart in the Highlands—or at any rate in Glasgow, or somewhere like that—his heart is certainly not here. He won't notice you much.'

'That is very soothing,' said Kit.

'You know, Dudley won't be jealous of you, as you're a temporary,' said Mary. 'But he may rather try to win your sympathy for his ideas.'

'I shall turn the conversation.'

'I'm afraid he'll try to use you,' said Mary. '"I wish, Christopher, you'd drop a hint to your good uncle" ... that sort of thing.'

'Yes,' said Kit. 'I can imagine that. Matron seems a nice comfortable soul. What about the other women?'

'Matron's all right, she's on our side,' said Mary. 'She's

9

a nice, wholesome woman who loves children, and she knows that's what the boys are. She takes thorns out of their fingers, and doses them, and tucks them up at night. She won't let anyone put any nonsense into their heads. For two pins, she'd tie a millstone round Dudley's neck, and push him in at the deep end of the swimming-bath.'

'Admirable woman!' said Kit. 'And the other two?'

'Oh, the blest pair of sirens?' said Mary. 'They are not with us, because they aspire to Dudley's hand: they want to be here, in my place.'

'Miss Rigby and Miss Hackett,' murmured Kit.

'We generally call Miss Hackett "Nan",' said Mary. 'Even the boys did, before Dudley stopped it. But we don't call Miss Rigby "Anita".'

'I should think not! What a name! Which of them do you back, Aunt Mary?'

'Oh, my dear, I'd rather hear your unbiased opinion on the matter; you'll soon have the chance of forming one.'

CHAPTER TWO

Ralph Wimbush and Harry Staples had both come back
with 'summer colds'; Matron discovered that they were a
little feverish, and put them in the sick-room.

'It's nice being let down gently like this,' said Harry.
'Not starting straight off with all the horrors of the
dorm.'

'But maddening our colds developed too late,' said
Ralph. 'We might have had another few days at home.'

'I was here any way; I mean, over at the Towers with
my aunt,' said Harry. 'I wouldn't want to be there any
longer; it's rather more peaceful here. Besides, I like
hearing bells, and knowing there's nothing one has to do
about them.'

'It's rather lovely,' said Ralph. 'And if my cold had
come on yesterday, I suppose I should only be in a
hotel. If I could be back in Uncle Bill Barchester's
villa on the Riviera, that would be super; worth it for
the food alone.'

'It's no worse here than at the Towers,' said Harry.
'It's better. Here it's good and plain; there it's just
plain, and rather lumpy.'

'My mater wouldn't put up with that,' said Ralph.
'She's a widow in reduced circumstances, but her friends
are good to her,' and unconsciously he reproduced one
of his mother's most captivating smiles. 'When we're on
our own (and that isn't very often) we can only afford to
have a woman in to clean and wash up; but the mater
has an account at a good shop, and we eat delicious

11

things out of tins and jars—and she's a good cook, when she feels like it.'

'At Aunt Hilda's a footman brings you watery potatoes, with blackheads in them, or whatever you call them,' said Harry. 'And in a silver dish.'

'Gracious, how nasty!' said Ralph, making a face. 'She's foreign too, isn't she? She ought to know better.'

'She's a Hun,' said Harry, incautiously. 'Of course she isn't a real relation,' he hurriedly put in. 'She's my Great-uncle's widow. It's all rather a long story.'

'Tell me, Harry,' said Ralph, stretching himself luxuriously.

But at that moment there was a voice at the door: 'Well, you young skrim-shankers; what have you to say for yourselves for slacking like this at the beginning of term?'

'We ought to be still at home, sir,' said Ralph. 'But we were so keen to get back to work that we came even in our interesting condition.'

'Ha, Wimbush, d'you want my other leg to pull?' said Dudley Knight, sitting on his bed.

'You're very severe, sir,' said Ralph, with a gesture that his mother might have used to make a guest feel at home.

'You, Staples, do look rather peaky,' said Dudley.

Harry's straight brown hair fell over his forehead, and he sat forward in bed with his hands clasped over his drawn-up knees. He, too, was like his mother; but she was an angular, shy, honest woman who had left his father (a colonel in India) because she found that she had come to dislike him so much. She now shared a house with another woman near the Welsh border, and was never spoken of by her husband's family; they would, indeed, have found it difficult to think of anything to say about her.

'We must have you both fit soon,' said Dudley, feeling

12

Ralph's shoulder muscles. Both boys wore the pink flannel jackets that were provided for the sick-room but, while Ralph seemed to be bursting opulently out of his, Harry's was too big, and the sleeves covered his hands.

'Get any bathing yet?' said Dudley to Ralph. 'Lucky chap, being in the south of France!'

'I went in once, but it was still pretty cold,' said Ralph.

'It's rather a late summer, isn't it, sir?' said Harry hopefully.

'Oh, it will warm up all right,' said Dudley heavily. 'We'll get the swimming-bath going in a week or two. Beastly rotten luck you had, last year, Staples, not being allowed to bathe. I asked your good aunt, and she seemed to think you'd be quite fit this term.'

'I suppose the doctor will say, sir,' said Harry, with resignation.

'He's a good chap, the old Doc,' said Dudley. 'But he's a bit old-fashioned. You must show him you're keen; let him see that you don't want to be coddled.'

'Mr Knight, where are your sick-room manners?' said a bright voice at the door. 'Sitting on a patient's bed! Don't you know it's against all the rules?'

'Oh, dear, Miss Hackett! Have I done something offside?' said Dudley, rising with a wouldbe humorous imitation of a guilty manner.

'Lucky for you it wasn't Matron who caught you,' said Nan Hackett.

'It would have been a hundred lines, I suppose,' said Dudley, grinning at the boys. 'Unless she sent me to the headmaster. Well, what do you think of these young slackers, taking to their beds as soon as they get back here?'

'I'm going to take their temps, then I'll know what to think,' said Nan efficiently. 'No, you needn't go, Mr Knight.'

'We'll both have to go in a minute,' he said.

'Well, we're not going to lose them just yet,' said Nan, shaking down the thermometers, 'Chicken for lunch, boys.'

'Chicken for lunch, indeed! We spoil them here, Miss Hackett,' said Dudley. 'What wonder if they go sick? When I was a boy at school...'

'Well, sir, there's been progress since then,' said Ralph.

'Hm, I wonder,' said Dudley, drawing a sigh that issued in a hiss.

But Matron came in, with Ronald Gibson. 'Company for you!' she said to the other boys, who looked at him in despair.

'So this is where you'd got to, Nan?' she continued. 'I was looking for you. Poor Ronald is feeling rather seedy; he's got a pain. Will you find Alice and tell her to bring a hot water-bottle?'

Dudley and Nan Hackett left the room. 'A hot water-bottle!' said Dudley. 'We'd have laughed at such a thing when I was at school.'

'You'd have been very wrong,' said Nan, in a prim little girl voice. 'It's a great comfort if you have a pain.'

'My dear Nan, boys have got to learn to bear a bit of pain,' said Dudley. 'D'you suppose they'll be coddled like this when they get to their public schools?'

'They'll be bigger boys then,' said Nan. 'And I suppose, even there, they'll be properly looked after when they're ill.'

'They'll have what's necessary, but no frills,' said Dudley. 'But they'll be with other boys who've been at schools very unlike this—do you want them to find themselves a laughing-stock?'

'Are other preparatory schools really so very different?' said Nan. 'The fees here are much the same as

14

at other schools round about; and I suppose we have to make a profit.'

Dudley looked at her sorrowfully. 'Ah, Nan, you don't think I grudge the boys proper food and shelter, I hope?'

'I didn't mean that.'

'Boys have got to learn to rough it a bit,' continued Dudley. And then Nan had to leave him, to go about her business.

'One doesn't usually take temperatures at this hour of the day,' said Harry. 'It's not as if we were awfully ill; she said we weren't.'

'She was just looking for an excuse to come in,' said Ralph. 'She must have seen Deadly Nightshade going along the passage.'

'She can't love that man!'

'I daresay she doesn't,' said Ralph. 'But he's her best chance; she wouldn't mind being headmaster's wife one day.'

'Ghastly the place would be, under those two,' said Harry. 'All draughts and heartiness, and smells of floor polish and boiled meat; and boys wearing their scout uniforms all the time.'

'Appalling,' said Ralph, 'I hope Dick and Mary will stay as long as we do; they probably will, as it's their home. Now, tell me all about your wicked German aunt.'

Harry gave a look at Ronald in the third bed.

'Don't bother about him,' said Ralph. 'He's probably asleep anyhow; and it's not as if it were anything for him to sneak to Matron about.'

Harry told the story, which was no unusual one: it gained considerably in the telling because he was fond of reading, and was of an age to enjoy the novels of great story-tellers. Ralph was an intelligent and flattering listener, and his questions suggested new possibilities.

'She's *nouveau riche* of course,' said Harry. 'What's that in the feminine?'

'*"Parvenue"*, I should think,' said Ralph. 'You mean your uncle was?'

It was admitted that the late Sir William (though of course he was a gentleman, having been the brother of Harry's grandmother) had not done at all badly out of the war. Such a thing might be said of the parents of a number of the boys, one or two of whom (though it was a school for the 'sons of gentlemen') were only moderately genteel. This, however, was a thing that the boys were told—false though they knew it to be—that 'one didn't talk about'. It was hoped that they would then not talk too much about it at home.

Sir William, on a business trip to the Continent soon after the war, had met this Central European widow; she was not 'pure Hun' but had mitigating strains of Czech and Hungarian blood. He was a widower, and he was won by her blandishments. Harry, with touches of Anthony Hope and Dumas, made her very much more fascinating than anyone who now knew her could easily believe. Ralph, less well read but more travelled, suggested a few other touches. Of course Sir William was infatuated, married her as fast as he could and brought her back to the Towers.

'And he turned his daughters out of the house,' said Harry. Then he had to admit that Cousin Rosa was, in fact, already married; but Cousin Mildred had very promptly decided to live with her sister.

Like his models, who were always willing to sacrifice character to plot, Harry now made a bold change in his picture of Aunt Hilda. Gone was the gipsy charm, the Zigeuner music (an interpolation of Ralph's); gone, even, was the suggestion of Jewish blood. What was left was a stiff, ugly martinet of a German governess, avid for money, and stingy about spending it.

16

'She always has a red nose, too,' said Harry, now relying upon observed fact, rather than hearsay or imagination.

'D'you think she drinks?' asked Ralph. 'Like Mr MacLeod?'

'I shouldn't be at all surprised,' said Harry gravely. 'But it may just be because the house is underheated; that's how I got my cold.'

'Or indigestion from the horrible food you told me about,' conjectured Ralph.

Then Harry went on to tell how completely Uncle William had been brought under her thumb, and how nasty she had been to Cousin Rosa or Cousin Mildred if they came over to luncheon. Finally, she got him to make a will in which she was left nearly everything—outright, too, and not just for her life—and the daughters had even been done out of family things, like their own mother's jewellery. Very soon afterwards Uncle William had died.

'Do you think there was foul play?' asked Ralph, delightedly.

'Well, it was all rather sudden,' said Harry. 'And none of the family was there at the time. Cousin Rosa did say she thought the doctor had muddled the case, but I never heard anyone suggest anything worse.'

'Of course, people have to be so careful what they say, because of the law,' said Ralph.

And now Aunt Hilda was reigning in solitary affluence and discomfort at the Towers. Harry's father (who had been away in India all the time, and did not know what a horrible woman she was—and it was to women that she showed her worse colours) liked him to stay there for a few days every holidays.

'Perhaps he hopes she'll leave you some of your uncle's money,' said Ralph. 'Or even the place.'

'I'd burn down the Towers, if she left me that awful house,' said Harry.

'You might get quite a good price for it,' said Ralph, in a more grownup tone. 'It could be turned into a school, or a private lunatic asylum.'

'No sane person would want to live in it,' said Harry.

'But of course, your aunt might marry again,' said Ralph. 'Did you notice, Deadly Nightshade was twining all round her yesterday, when she brought you back?'

'That would be one in the eye for Nan,' said Harry.

'And for Miss Rigby.'

'Is she after him too?' asked Harry.

'Don't you notice anything?' said Ralph, with scorn. 'I wonder if Dudley has a chance with your aunt. Awful for you; he'd be your uncle.'

'Hardly,' said Harry. 'We might drop Aunt Hilda then.'

'And he might give up the school,' said Ralph. 'That would be wonderful. But I don't know what he'd find to do. Perhaps your aunt could get him made a bishop.'

'Could she?'

'It depends on how much money she's got,' said Ralph. 'Money can do anything. Then he'd be called "Me Lud".'

' "Me Lud Dud",' said Harry, and they both laughed.

'I think he'd enjoy telling people not to call him "My Lord",' said Ralph. 'He'd be "so simple".'

But Ronald stirred, heaved and groaned, raised himself up, and was violently sick into the wash-basin by his bed.

'Ugh!' said Ralph.

'I think I brought a little up,' said Ronald.

CHAPTER THREE

' "The casement slowly grows a glimmering square",' said Michael Park. They had learned that poem last term for repetition.

It had been light for some time, but the windows of the Grey Room were overshadowed by trees.

'I hate "the early pipe of half-awakened birds",' said Harry Staples.

'Ah!' said Michael with satisfaction, as a screech from the kitchen cat silenced the birds' cacophony.

A maid clattered in with a tray of milk, and banged down thick white mugs beside Ralph Wimbush, Harry Staples and Ronald Gibson, who were supposed to require it.

'Ugh!' said Ralph, dabbling in it with his fingers to pull out the skin.

' "Pampered brutes!" As Deadly Nightshade would say,' said Michael.

'I wish Deadly had had to drink this muck when he was at school,' said Harry. 'D'you think I could chuck it in my po, and say: "please, Matron, I think I've brought a little up"?'

'You'd be found out and swished,' said Tony Stuart. 'Or Matron would dose you with something just as foul.'

'I should chuck it out of the window,' said Michael. 'I'll open it and see. It ought to fall into the bushes all right.'

'Park, you're head of the room,' said George Girling

disapprovingly. 'You ought to keep order. You shouldn't encourage them to waste good food.'

'My name's Michael.'

'It's Park, too.'

'One's name is anything one may be called, George,' said Michael. 'One of your names is Girlie.'

'If you think it's good food, George, have my milk,' said Ralph.

'No, it's your business to drink it, and get strong and fit,' said George.

Michael took the two mugs, and hurled the contents well out of the window.

'Ronald's drinking his!' said Ralph.

'Snakes like milk,' said Harry. 'I read that in the encyclopaedia.'

The bell rang, authorizing them to talk, and ordering them to rise.

'Well, who's got German aunts?' taunted Ronald.

'Only one; and she's not really an aunt and not completely a German,' said Harry.

'But nearly an aunt, and partly a German,' said Ronald. 'He said so, didn't he, Ralph?'

'I don't think he said so to you,' said Ralph.

'So you're partly a Hun?' said George. 'Harry the Hun!'

'Stow it, George,' said Ralph. 'The King's got German aunts.'

'I don't think you should say that,' said George, trying to look down his nose with disapproval, a thing that he found difficult to do, as it turned up violently.

'If he has, it's bad luck on him,' said Hugh Tupholme.

'Well, Harry didn't choose his aunts any more than the King,' said Michael.

'She's only an aunt by marriage,' said Harry.

'Harry's got no German blood,' said Ralph.

'D'you mean the King has?' asked George, in a threatening tone.

'You're very noisy this morning, boys,' said Matron, coming in on the course of her rounds. 'What's the argument about?'

'Whether the King has German blood,' said Michael.

'We don't talk about it,' said Matron. 'I daresay many people have, if the truth were known.'

'But we have to talk about it; it's in History,' said Michael. 'The Hanoverians, and all that.'

'Well, leave it to your History lesson, and get on with your dressing,' said Matron. 'Any boy not dressed by silence time gets a conduct mark.'

'Silence time' was the last five minutes before the bell. All round the room boys went down on their knees, by their unmade beds, and said their morning prayers. Then they sat on their chairs and had to learn their 'verses'. The first lesson of the day was given up to reciting these (bit by bit they learned the epistle for the following Sunday), and then other Scripture was read.

Mr Langton was not in a very good temper. 'Ridiculous, boys of your age stumbling over a few verses in English,' he said. 'I've a good mind to make you learn them in Greek, in future.'

As only a few boys learned Greek (and it was not Mr Langton's own subject), this threat caused no great dismay.

He quickly regained his temper, as they read some Old Testament History; he was apt to identify himself with Jehovah, whom, indeed, he imitated in public life with a fair degree of success.

The whole school and all the staff assembled in the big classroom for prayers.

Mr Langton read them a passage from the book of Numbers.

'Let us pray,' said the Reverend Dudley Knight in his

turn. Down they all went on their knees, with the soles of their shoes turned towards the middle of the room. He had led them in the Lord's Prayer (supplying the expression), and then (with yet more expression) he read one of Stevenson's prayers: 'O Lord, we thank Thee that Thou art no hard taskmaster, grimly watching the stint of work we bring...'

Mrs Langton announced a hymn, *Crown Him with many crowns,* and struck a chord. She at least had gauged the boys' tastes, for they sang it with gusto:

> *ff Creator of the ro-holling spheres,*
> *Ineffably sublime.*

'I think religious exercise ought to aim at getting up an appetite for breakfast,' she murmured to Kit, as the two of them walked in the rear of the procession to the dining-room.

'I didn't like Dudley's prayer,' said Kit.

'No, it sounded like a disloyal criticism of your uncle,' said Mary. 'Fortunately it was flatly contradicted by the lesson, if they listened to that.'

'They followed it in their Bibles,' said Kit. 'It had a better chance than the prayer.'

'But they hear that prayer quite often.'

The Grey Room boys, the junior half of the sixth form, sat at the bottom of the headmaster's table. George Girling owed the position to his age, and length of time at school; the others were young and clever, except for Ronald Gibson, who was betwixt and between.

Intellectual inequality was levelled, to some extent, by a spelling game in the Morse code, which Mr Langton had instituted in order to practise them in that accomplishment.

'Dot dash,' said the head-boy, on his right, and returned to his kedgeree.

'Dash dot dot dot,' said the boy next him.

'Dot,' contributed Michael Park, and so it went on till it got to Ronald Gibson.

'Dot,' he said, as the safest bid.

'Challenge you!' said someone from the opposite side of the table. And he did not know what word he was trying to spell; he could not even spell out the word as far as they had got.

Mr Langton flushed a deep red. 'If you can't learn the Morse code, you'd better sit at the baby table till you can,' he blustered.

For the first hour they had Latin, with Mr Knight; the second book of the Aeneid.

'*Conticuere omnes*, they all shut up, and that's what I'd like you to do,' said Dudley, who rather liked making the classics, 'Virgil and all those fellows', talk in our own language.

'Go on, Wimbush.'

'*Infandum, regina, iubes renovare dolorem,*' read Ralph. 'Ma'am, does Your Majesty command me to renew an unspeakable grief?'

'You dare to call Dido "ma'am"!' said Dudley.

There was a splutter of laughter.

'Oh, sir, I thought you liked us to use ordinary language,' said Ralph. 'That's how one talks to a queen.'

'And when have you talked to a queen?'

'Last holidays, sir,' said Ralph demurely. 'The ex-queen of Ruthenia came to tea at my uncle Barchester's villa.'

'Well, the rest of us don't move in such exalted circles,' said Dudley with sarcasm. 'Let's hear your version of the line, Park?'

'Queen, it is an unspeakable grief that you order me to renew,' said Michael.

'Good, good; you get the meaning, though you are

taking a liberty with the syntax,' said Dudley. 'And "Queen" is a bit bald. "My Queen" or "O Queen" perhaps. Let us try to put it into dignified English. "Sovereign Lady, thou bidst me renew a grief unspeakable." Can we improve on that?' he ended, as if satisfied that no further improvement was possible.

'Ineffable,' suggested Harry.

'That's a wretched, finicking sort of a word,' said Dudley. 'Where did you get hold of a word like that?'

'It was in the hymn, sir,' said Harry. ' "Ineffably sublime".'

'Why do they make you fellows sing rot like that?' said Dudley, and soon he was well away in his indignation against *Hymns Ancient and Modern*, to the comfort of those who had not well prepared their construe lesson.

One by one, boys had timidly asked to be 'excused'; but now they did not venture to interrupt Dudley's discourse. Finally Miss Rigby made an incursion.

'I beg your pardon, Mr Knight,' she said. 'I came to ask for Tony Stuart, for his music lesson.'

'Why did you keep a lady waiting?' asked Dudley. 'Cut along now.'

'I'm sorry, Miss Rigby,' said Tony. 'Mr Knight was being so interesting that I quite forgot the time.'

Tony was very pretty, and had already discovered the disarming effect of his smiles.

'I shall have a bone to pick with you, Mr Knight, if you make my pupils forget me like this,' said Miss Rigby.

'Ah, you will be able to get even with me, Miss Rigby,' said Dudley. 'Never fear that.'

Ralph and Harry gave each other significant looks during this interchange, and Harry had to look into his desk to hide a fit of the giggles.

'Tony wasn't late by my watch,' said Ralph, on their way to the next lesson. 'Miss Rigby was just inventing an excuse to come in. You saw how she enjoyed it?'

They entered the headmaster's classroom, then all smiles stopped together.

Exercises had been given back, and they were not very good.

'Heartless, heartless class!' lamented Mr Langton.

Then he went round the room, giving what he called 'individual attention'; this normally took the form of physical violence.

He began on Ronald Gibson. 'What's this mess, boy?' Ronald produced an unsatisfactory explanation. The true explanation was obvious: he had looked up the answer to his sum at the back of the book, but his working of it out justified no such conclusion.

'Dewlaps!' growled the headmaster. He gripped the boy by the throat, just beneath the chin, and swung him vigorously to and fro.

Finally the child gave a choking gulp, and Mr Langton released him, fearing, perhaps, that he was going to be sick.

'Your father told me to keep an eye on you, and I shall keep both eyes on you,' said Mr Langton to the sobbing boy. 'And if you get up to any more of these shifty games, I'll beat you. No, I won't: you shall have six of the best from the gardener, who's a stronger man than I am.'

'Now it's your turn,' said the headmaster, coming to George Girling.

'Sir, I did it by algebra,' said George.

'Oh, you did it by algebra, did you!' said Mr Langton. 'Let me just get you by the short hairs!'

He did so.

'Though you're big enough to have whiskers,' said Mr Langton (tugging and twisting the short hair in front of

George's right ear), 'you don't know as much algebra as any boy in the fourth form.'

'And that goes for you, too, Hugh,' he said to the next boy.

He now took up a position between the two desks, and gripping one boy by an ear, and the other by his hair, he banged their heads rhythmically together and chanted the formula.

'(a plus b) squared [bang] is *not* a squared plus b squared [bang] but a squared [bang] plus 2 ab [bang] plus b squared [bang]. I hope I've knocked that into your heads!'

He then went to the blackboard and worked out the sum in beautifully written numbers, and with complete lucidity; and calm seemed to be restored, until Ronald Gibson asked if he might leave the room.

There was another explosion of temper, for the headmaster (like Jehovah) had sanitary laws that must be observed.

'You had all the first hour to go in,' he exclaimed. 'It stands to reason that you go as soon after breakfast as you can. You don't want all that disgusting muck fermenting in you all day; you're poisoning the air....'

Miss Rigby stood, transfixed, at the door.

'You're a walking manure-heap,' continued the headmaster. 'A dung-cart; go and empty yourself!'

Miss Rigby asked if she could have Hugh Tupholme for his music lesson.

'Oh, Miss Rigby, you're welcome to what's left of him,' said the headmaster. 'He's done no good here.'

After this lesson there was break. Matron issued towels and bathing-drawers, and most of the school went to the swimming-bath (Kit Henderson in charge). Those who, for one reason or another, were not allowed to bathe that day went out in front of the house, where

Miss Rigby put them through a little half-hearted Swedish drill. Mr Langton emerged through a french window, carrying a backless bench.

'Now, come here; you, Harry Staples; you, Alan Dearden; you, Frank Goodbody,' he said. 'You've not passed your swimming tests; let's see how you make your strokes.'

In turn, they balanced precariously with their stomachs on the bench, and tried to cleave the air with their arms. Mr Langton came round, and sometimes worked their legs for them.

'Slowly,' he said. 'In time with your breath. Bring your legs together, and then kick out hard. Not bad; no reason why you shouldn't all swim perfectly.'

They had to go in, to more milk; but this time it was cold, and everyone had to drink it. One might pour a little of one's own into emptied mugs. Moreover there were biscuits, and these were dry, and needed washing down.

The last hour of the morning was spent with Mr MacLeod. That gloomy and misanthropic person (who drank a good deal of whisky at night in his room) had not yet managed to shave. He now proceeded unsteadily to do this (most imperfectly concealed behind the blackboard), while the class was told to read the History book. They were in the Wars of the Roses, a period which, by mismanagement, many of them had lately done in the fifth form. St Albans, Barnet, Northampton ... they memorized. It was, apparently, important to know the order of the battles, though one need attach no geographical ideas to the place names, nor need one know the dates, or who won or lost. 'Hedgley Moor, Hexham, Towton' ... but surely something had been left out?

Mr MacLeod had a contempt for English History before the Union, and was easily satisfied.

They assembled in the big classroom, to walk in

decorously to school dinner: soup, roast mutton or haricot mutton, treacle pudding. Mr Langton, occupied with carving, set the boys at his table to play a guessing game, one side against the other.

The boy on his left announced that he was a scriptural character.

'Are you in the Old Testament?'

'No.'

'Are you in the Acts?'

'Yes.'

'Are you a man?'

'No.'

'Are you a good character?'

'No.'

This was too easy.

'Are you Sapphira?'

'Yes.'

After school dinner there was a brief half hour when the bigger boys had a moment to themselves; the younger children had to rest on their beds; but their seniors, plunged in Dumas or Anthony Hope or Rider Haggard forgot the school and the whispering beech trees outside and in their happy trance saw the court of Louis XIII, or a Greek island, or the shores of Africa.

The sixth form, now with Kit Henderson, had to wake up to the life of a French village. A large picture was hung up, and a simple conversation of question and answer was attempted. 'Alan, Daniel, Guy, Michel, Antoine, Henri, Rodolphe, Georges, Hugues' and one or two others had to account for everyone in the village, and his occupation.

'What is Monsieur le Curé doing?'

'He is reading his prayer book.'

'Why is he reading it in the street?'

'He is on the way to visit a sick person.'

'What is the baker's boy doing?'

'He is carrying loaves of bread.'

'Do they look good?' asked Kit, an unexpected question.

'They look delicious,' said Ralph. 'I wish we had bread like that.'

'What is the butcher's boy doing?'

'He is carrying a tray of meat.'

'What are the dogs doing?'

'They are fighting over a bone.'

'What is the time?'

'Half past nine by the church clock.'

Here it was the sleepy hour of half past three.

The fifth lesson, before tea, was quiet but of fearful moment. They sat doing algebra problems for the headmaster, and these would come up for judgement the next day. Meanwhile he sat peacefully at his desk, giving an occasional snort of contempt as he corrected the work of other boys. Finally, in a genial mood, he told them that tea would be in the garden.

This was a pleasant custom of the summer term. Trestle tables were brought out on to a sunk lawn, and the boys ate their meal seated on forms, or on the bank, under the murmuring silken leaves of the beech trees. There was a relaxation of discipline. It was thought too hot a day to force boys to eat more than they really wanted.

Cricket followed. Kit was umpire in the junior game, in which 'rabbits' like Michael Park, Harry Staples and Ralph Wimbush played. They had contrived to be on the same side, but on this afternoon they had the bad luck to be fielding, and were dispersed at far points.

Their only exercise was crossing at the end of every over. They passed, meeting on the pitch, pausing as long as they dared to exchange lively gestures of boredom and despair. Towards the end of their ordeal, Harry was hit on the shoulder by a ball, which he had not seen in time to avoid. Kit stopped the play for a few minutes and took him to the pavilion, where Matron opened a bottle of witch hazel to apply some to his bruise, and the room was filled with the most delicious smell in the world.

Kit walked up with him and Michael at the end of play.

'You see, Harry,' he said, 'we schoolmasters aren't being quite such fools as you think, when we say life is like a game of cricket. It is very dangerous to let yourself get so bored that you don't notice what is going on. Something hard may come and hit you, before you've time to get out of the way.'

The boys laughed with appreciation.

'That's not really supposed to be the way to play cricket,' said Michael.

'Isn't it? I've mercifully forgotten,' said Kit. 'Of course I could draw quite another moral, I suppose. You're at the edge of the field—not because you aren't much good, and frankly don't care a button—but because it's an honourable and dangerous position, like being on the frontiers of the Empire. And you save the day by a brilliant catch....'

'That sounds rather like a sermon by Mr Knight,' said Harry demurely.

'But quite unlike it, I'm sure,' said Kit briskly, hastening the pace. There was supper: bread and butter, and very good fresh lemonade. For the sixth form there was also prep: Latin sentences for Dudley Knight. Then there were prayers.

And the morning and the evening were another day.

CHAPTER FOUR

On Sunday a thunderstorm was clearing the heavy air; meanwhile it kept them from walking to the village church. The morning service for the day was read; boys chosen by the headmaster read the first and second lessons appointed in the prayer book. The Reverend Dudley Knight gave a short address, of which it may suffice to quote the peroration.

'The one thing that matters is to keep a straight bat, and to take one's share of the bowling without complaint. You'll find that Life can send down some pretty hard balls; and sometimes they break in surprising ways. You have to be ready for them. To some of you there may come a grand moment, when you hit the ball well over the pavilion: may it be so. And may it leave you without swelled heads. Sometimes, in life, the Captain wants us to play a sporting game; sometimes He just wants us to stall. It's for us to try to find out His will, and to do it.

'And the end? Well, we know there'll be some chaps in at the end of play, when the Skipper declares, and they'll carry their bats. But we must face the fact that almost certainly our wicket will fall, in one way or another. In one way Life is not like cricket; there's no tallywag, and we shan't know our score. But, be our innings short or long—whether we're caught, or bowled or stumped—may it be the lot of each of us, when he reaches the pavvy, to hear the Skipper say: "Well played!"'

The boys had been allowed to choose their own hymns, and they liked them sugary:

p Angels of Jesus!(cr) Angels of night,
f Singing to welcome(p) the pilgrims of the night!

The weather cleared in time for an afternoon walk. This was led, rather rapidly for short legs, by the headmaster, and Kit was in attendance.

'Will you walk with me?' said Ralph.

'Yes, please,' said Harry.

'You'd rather walk with Tony,' said Ralph, without jealousy.

'No,' said Harry.

'Liar; I heard you ask him first,' said Ralph.

'Well he's engaged,' said Harry. 'He's walking with Guy.'

'Of course, he's pretty, if you like that sort of face,' said Ralph.

'Most people do.'

'I daresay you're right,' said Ralph. 'I don't find it very interesting myself; and I don't find him very interesting either. But nice, of course.'

'As nice as Ronald's beastly.'

'No one's as nice as all that,' said Ralph. 'Ronald's walking with George Girling. Who else would have either of them?'

'Hugh often walks with George.'

'Perhaps he's got left over; he'll have to walk with Dick Langton.'

'Who's got German aunts?' cried Ronald's voice.

'No one you know,' said Harry.

'Liar,' said Ronald. 'Harry the Hun has.'

'Who's he?'

'Thou art the man!' said George.

'I'm not a Hun; I have only one great-aunt by marriage, who's partly German.'

'Not very patriotic of your great-uncle to marry her,' said George judicially. 'You'd better keep her dark when you get to your public school.'

'He can't; I'm going to Slowborough, too,' said Ronald.

'If you pass,' said Ralph; not a very effective shot, for Ronald was not quite so stupid as all that.

'Harry thinks she got hold of his uncle and made him leave her everything he had,' chirped Ronald, dancing on his toes. 'And then he thinks there may have been foul play.'

'If he thinks that, he ought to tell someone,' said George solemnly. 'He can't leave it like that. If he won't tell the Dud, I shall.'

'Oh, go away, and mind your own business, George!' said Harry.

'Murder is everyone's business,' said George righteously. 'A good citizen is bound to report a crime, if he knows about it.'

'But I knew nothing about it!' screamed Harry, at the end of his tether.

'Then you've invented it,' said Ronald. 'You've made up stories against your aunt's character; and that's a crime—even if she's a Hun.'

'It's not like that,' said Harry.

'Well, it must be one way or the other,' said George. 'I think the Dud ought to be told about it any way.'

'But Harry thinks the Dud wants to marry her!' screamed Ronald with malice.

Harry rushed at him with open hands.

'Scratch, do you?' said George.

'You two are being a nuisance,' said Kit, drawing near to George and Ronald. 'You'd better walk on and leave

Ralph and Harry alone. You're more bother than you're worth.'

'But sir, he shouldn't say that Mr Knight...'

'You shouldn't tell me what he says about another master,' said Kit. 'I refuse to hear it. Run along, as I told you.'

They walked a little in silence.

'What was he tormenting you about?' said Kit.

'Oh, nothing, sir.'

'You mean, you don't want to tell me,' said Kit. 'All right for now. But if there's any more nonsense of the sort you must. I'll put an end to it.'

'He's going on to the same public school as me,' said Harry, dolefully.

'What, Ronald? All the more reason to shut him up, and take no nonsense from him,' said Kit. 'I don't know what all this is about, Harry; and I don't want to, except to stop it. But I'll tell you one thing; nothing will be carried on from here to your next school.'

'Really, sir?'

'No one will be in the slightest bit interested in prep school stories,' said Kit. 'Besides, you'll pass in so much higher than Ronald that you'll leave him behind at once. You're not going to the same house, I hope?'

'I don't know, sir.'

'Find that out; it might be changed. Any way, we might send you in for a scholarship at some other school. In any case, you can forget all about Ronald.'

'But won't a public school be *worse*, sir?' said Harry.

Like every boy at Hazelcroft he was constantly hearing about the life of the world to come. This (for those not destined to the Royal Navy) was in every case a public school. Most of them expected it to be Purgatory. To bold spirits like George Girling it sounded like Heaven. Harry, and others like him, expected Hell.

'Worse than here, d'you mean?' said Kit. 'D'you think

34

that's a polite thing to say to a master? This place isn't so bad, you know.'

'Sorry, sir,' said Harry. 'I didn't mean that.'

'Well, I'm sorry; I didn't mean to tease you,' said Kit. 'But you and Ralph are among the few boys capable of being articulate; and one ought to make you express yourselves properly, don't you agree?'

'Yes, sir,' said Ralph.

'Shan't I have a worse time at a public school?' asked Harry. 'Everyone says so.'

'I've never said so,' said Kit. 'Who's everyone?'

'Masters, other boys, Miss Hackett...'

'Well, the other boys haven't been to a public school yet, and Miss Hackett didn't go to a boys' school. The masters might be wrong, you know.'

'They hadn't always been to a public school,' said Ralph with malice.

'It depends on luck and on the school,' said Kit. 'But I should think in any public school there are one or two advantages, that perhaps you haven't thought of.'

'What, sir?'

'Well, among five hundred boys you're not so much noticed as you are among fifty,' said Kit. 'I don't think you want to be exactly like everyone else; it will be a little easier to be yourself in such a crowd. Though not very, I'm afraid.'

'I thought the public schools tried to turn out a type, sir,' said Ralph.

'Oh, I suppose they do,' said Kit. 'I know people have talked about them as if they were sausage machines. But the machinery is faulty, thank God. Some real people come out of public schools. And some boys might just as well be made into sausages, don't you think?'

'Like George Girling,' said Ralph.

'We won't mention names,' said Kit. 'Then, at a

35

public school you'll have much more time to yourselves; I should think you'd like that.'

'I should!' said Harry. 'We have so little here.'

'Then, there's another thing that you'd hardly understand yet,' said Kit. 'At any good public school there must be a few men with first class brains, teaching the sixth forms. You'll be able to talk to them about anything that's important to you, as if they were real human beings, not just schoolmasters—at least, I hope so. They ought to leaven the lump a bit; I mean, a society of about six hundred people must be a bit different from what it would otherwise be, if there are six or more first class men in it.'

'But aren't there first class men here, sir?' said Ralph. 'Mr Langton?'

'We won't make any comparisons,' said Kit. 'My uncle is, indeed, a very able man; I am sure he could have done brilliantly at the University if he'd chosen. But he was well off, and did just what he liked, and took a pass degree, and travelled....'

'Well, we've got you, sir,' said Ralph, clutching his arm affectionately.

'That's nice of you, Ralph,' said Kit. 'And I couldn't teach at a public school till I've been through Cambridge. But the thing about me is, I've been at a public school quite lately, and remember exactly what it was like. I'm very glad it's over; but it was quite tolerable.'

'Not "the best time of your life", sir?' said Ralph.

'I should think not! I've been very happy since, in France and Italy. But I wasn't miserable at school; at least not very often, or for very long at a time.'

'I suppose you were good at games, sir?' asked Harry.

'Not more than average,' said Kit. 'But you shouldn't make games such a bugbear. People at school are more practical about them than you'd think; there's nothing special or sacred about them.'

'I've heard people say they were a sort of religion,' said Ralph.

'And Mr Knight's sermons...' began Harry.

'I expect Mr Knight chooses illustrations from games, because he wants everyone to understand him,' said Kit tactfully. 'On the whole, you'll find people are reasonable. If you're good at games, they'll take trouble with you, and bring you on; because they hope you'll do credit to your house or the school.'

'That won't happen to either of us,' said Harry.

'No, but you needn't be superior about people who are good,' Kit warned him. 'Someone like Tony Stuart, who plays a very pretty innings, isn't to be despised.'

'Tony is a very pretty boy,' said Ralph.

'Perhaps too much for his happiness,' said Kit. 'It might be a good thing if he broke his nose—but don't say I said so. We said we'd avoid personalities.'

'But if you're not good at games?' Harry went on.

'If you're just average, like me, you rub along somehow,' said Kit. 'If you're really hopeless, they haven't time for you, and you don't often have to play. Any way, there aren't always games for everyone every day.'

'Really!' said Harry, a smile of beatitude spreading over his face.

'No,' said Kit. 'In the winter terms they generally make you take some form of exercise every day; but as often as not you'll just go for a run, I expect.'

'That must be a strain at first,' said Ralph. 'One's wind ...'

'Oh, you don't have to tear along, as if it was the hundred yards,' said Kit. 'A slow jog trot will do; and you can drop out and tie up your shoe, if you don't do it too often.'

'You take a load off one's mind, sir,' said Harry gratefully.

'And there's one more thing I should like you to

37

remember,' said Kit. 'You've both got very much more brains than the average boy. You, Ralph, ought to pass in at least half way up the school, wherever you go; and you, Harry, ought to pass in even higher. You won't be like little boys going into the first or second form here; you'll go in with two hundred and fifty boys below you.'

'Does that make much difference, sir; outside lessons, I mean?' asked Harry.

'It makes a great deal of difference,' said Kit. 'You'll start already with some privileges, and you'll soon get more. And in two years or less you'll be in the sixth, and everyone will have to treat you as if you were a human being.'

'And we're told only games matter!' said Harry.

'Oh, they matter too,' said Kit. 'They improve your social life, so to speak. You're allowed to wear a lot of special ties and scarves and caps, and little boys think you're a tin god; and masters will let you down as easily as they can. It's probably all great fun while it lasts. But if you're a brainless lout it doesn't last. If you don't make enough progress in work they get rid of you: it's called "superannuation". Boys who pass in low are always in danger of it.'

After tea, Mrs Langton read to them in the drawing-room. The fire had been lit, a cheering sight on a damp day. They sat on the floor; toffee had been handed round, and each of them had a bit in either cheek. The lamplight fell in a small circle round Mrs Langton and her book, and (to the satisfaction of many eyes), it shone also on the delightful head of Tony Stuart, whom she had placed at her knee.

The book from which she read had been chosen from the school library several terms ago. These readings were not at all regular, and probably no one there could have given a synopsis of the previous events; but it was the sort of boys' book that just goes on and on. The title (which was unpromising) was *The Middy of the Blunderbore*; an assistant matron had picked out the book as likely to encourage naval vocations among the boys.

This evening's portion had no tiresome nautical language, and indeed had a situation that a good novelist could have made something of. The hero (for some reason, doubtless explained in previous chapters) was either temporarily or permanently very deaf, and for other reasons, no doubt excellent, he was trying to conceal this defect. This made him a blunderer indeed, but he was not boring.

Sunday ended with hymns of their own choosing.

The day Thou gavest, Lord, is ended ...

CHAPTER FIVE

'Scratching! Like a girl!' said George Girling. 'What would your father say, if he heard you scratched.'

'I don't know him very well,' said Harry. 'But I should hope he would be sorry that I was driven to it.'

'I expect he'd take you away from school,' said George.

'That wouldn't break my heart,' said Harry. 'I could have a tutor.'

'Very expensive,' said Ronald Gibson. 'More likely you'd be sent to one of those schools for Backward and Delicate Boys.'

'There are some backward boys here,' said Ralph Wimbush.

'Stow it, Wimbush,' said George, showing a clenched fist. 'How Harry thinks he's going to get on at a public school...'

'I might not go to one,' said Harry. 'As you say, there are other schools.'

George gasped, as if he had heard a blasphemy.

'But you have to!' he said. 'One has to be a public school man.'

'I see no necessity,' said Harry.

'I'm sure your father will insist on it,' said George.

'You'd better think about passing the Common Entrance exam, George,' said Michael Park. 'If you fail, you won't get into a public school, not even if your father insists till he's blue in the face.'

'They may not accept Harry, if he has a German aunt,' said Ronald.

'All the better,' said Harry. 'But I'm afraid—fools though they probably are—they're not such big fools as all that.'

'Some parents might not like to send their boys to school with a boy who had German relations,' said George pompously.

'Particularly if she's a murderess,' said Ronald.

'Oh, shut up!' said Harry.

Then Nan Hackett came in to see if they were ready, for it lacked a minute to silence time.

'Why do you let George and Ronald torment Harry like this?' she asked Michael Park.

'He sticks up for himself better than you think, Miss Hackett,' said Michael. 'And they'll soon get tired of it.'

'But what's it about?'

'Oh, it's only rot,' he said, knowing that she did not believe him.

'I'm not sure that I ought to leave it like this,' said Nan doubtfully. Then she announced silence, and Harry was as safe as if he were in sanctuary, while prayers were said and Bibles thumbed.

The third lesson was taken by Miss Rigby: a singing lesson for the whole school.

Kit walked in the garden, being free like the rest of the staff. At the moment it was most beautiful: lilac trees, white and mauve, were in flower, and great azalea bushes blazed. Even though to his eyes (lately accustomed to the south) the slates and gables of the house and its sash windows, emphasized by white paint, were supremely hideous, and much as he detested the virginia creeper, he could always turn his back on it. He buried his nose in a golden scented azalea, and listened to the fresh young voices coming from the big classroom. They were singing a sea-shanty.

As I was a-walking down Winchester street—
Give me way—blow the man down!
A saucy young lassie I happened to meet—
Oh—give me some time to blow the man down!

Then there was a line on the piano.

Said I: 'Pretty Polly, and how do you do?'
Give me way—blow the man down!
Said she: 'None the better for seeing of you!'
Oh—give me some time to blow the man down!

'Such pleasant smells and sounds in the garden, Aunt Mary!' said Kit to his aunt, who was in the hall pouring out mid-morning coffee for the staff. 'But your coffee smells as good as anything.'

'There's no point in coffee if it's not good,' said Mary Langton. 'One's been in houses where they give you black broth. I don't want any Spartan touch here.'

Dudley Knight frowned, as he moved over into a corner with Nan Hackett.

'I expect in Sparta they enjoyed thinking themselves very high-minded for not complaining about the food,' said Kit. 'You rob people of that pleasure.'

'I hope so,' she said. 'I can't bear that form of self-righteousness. If food is nasty, people ought to complain.'

'Or just leave the stuff,' said Kit.

'Well, if the Helots had left their black broth, they'd have had to give them something better,' said Mary. 'They couldn't starve them; they needed their slave labour.'

'And I must be off to mine,' said Kit. 'I'm "baths-master" or whatever you call it. At least the Spartans had no such person. I bet none of them could swim.'

The bath was a dank-looking oblong, screened by bushes on two sides; at the shallow end was a wooden shelter with pegs to hold the boys' clothes. They faced it modestly while they undressed. On the third side was a fence, behind which quiet cows munched the grass. When Kit blew his whistle, the boys were allowed to enter the bath (and indeed must do so with no great delay); when it blew again, they must get out.

He watched them get in, in their different ways. Timid boys lowered themselves in at the shallow end, holding on at the edge and slipping forward. Others jumped in, about half-way, and splashed about. A few good swimmers, like Ralph Wimbush, dived in neatly at the deep end. But for all of them one rite was compulsory: each boy had to duck his head at once, for fear of sun-stroke. A little while in the south had taught Kit to smile at this quaint English superstition. It reigned supreme at Hazelcroft; the boys never went out in summer without great mushroom-shaped flannel hats to protect them from the pale sun of Surrey.

Today the headmaster had come down to look at the scene.

'Very pretty dive, Ralph,' he said. 'You've got to do something about your dive, George. Hitting the water smack with your stomach!'

He looked with approval at the boys in the middle, who were at least trying, and sometimes got their feet off the bottom.

At the shallow end, boys gripping the side and waiting for the whistle to allow them to clamber out on to dry ground, timidly advanced a pace or two across the slippery floor. Mr Langton was quite capable of poking them away from their place of safety with a pole; moreover, at the other end of this pole, hung a canvas belt, and only bold spirits would care to be taken in it for a swimming lesson. Harry looked at him, and made a few correct breast strokes, but he was careful not to move his feet.

'You won't get far that way!' said Mr Langton, with a laugh. 'Remind me to put you in the belt next time.'

Mr MacLeod, for once in a happy state of drink, was giving them an English lesson. He did not think much of the anthology of poems provided by the school. It had been bought twenty years ago, and the copies would be hired out to boys every term until they fell to pieces. He dictated to them, influenced in his choice, perhaps, by the lovely morning.

> *On a day, alack the day!*
> *Love, whose month was ever May,*
> *Spied a blossom passing fair*
> *Playing in the wanton air.*
> *Through the velvet leaves the wind*
> *All unseen gan passage find,*
> *And the lover, sick to death,*
> *Wished himself the heaven's breath:*
> *'Air', quoth he, 'thy cheeks may blow;*
> *Air, that I might triumph so.'*

It was perhaps as well that Mr MacLeod's whisky breath was limited in its range and triumph. The boys could not smell it, nor did the Glaswegian accent destroy the beauty of the poem for those who could feel it.

> *Thrü the velvet leaves the waynd*
> *All unseen garn parsage faynd,*

Mr MacLeod repeated. And Guy Tracy gasped with a hitherto unknown pain, as a butterfly hovered over Tony Stuart's head.

All very well for Shakespeare, thought Harry Staples, who perceived the lines to be most beautiful, but knew they would provide no help when he was in the dank bath, dangling from the headmaster's pole. Shakespeare, someone had told him, had probably not been able to swim. It was hardly likely that he had ever tried, or that he had been completely immersed in water since the day of his baptism. If one had lived in those days, one might have liked May well enough; now it was a pleasure in September to pick blackberries round the dry bath, whose bottom was then covered with fallen leaves.

'Mr Knight, may I have a word with you?' said Nan Hackett, when the staff were drinking coffee in the hall, after the school dinner.

'As many as you like, dear Nan.'

'It's about that poor child, Harry Staples; I found him crying in the boot-room.'

'Crying at his age!' said Dudley. 'Is someone dead?'

'No, he's just so terrified,' said Nan. 'Mr Langton said he was going to put him in the belt for a swimming-lesson.'

'Very good of the headmaster,' said Dudley. 'Do him good, the little funk.'

'Mr Knight, he's a nervous child,' said Nan. 'He's afraid he'll lose his head and do all his strokes wrong; and (you won't mind my saying it) the headmaster can get a little impatient at times.'

'The headmaster is a fine teacher.'

'I know,' said Nan. 'But you can't teach swimming the same way as you teach Arithmetic.'

'Boys have got to learn both.'

'Need they all?' pleaded Nan. 'On the Continent, I believe, many boys don't ever learn; and in England I don't think the lower classes always do.'

'Staples has been entered for an English public school, Nan,' said Dudley. 'It will be worse for him if he arrives there and can't swim.'

'I'm not sure that anything can be worse for him,' said

Nan. 'The boy is scared out of his mind; he'll never learn here. Do boys ever learn here, any way? They're only in for a few minutes, and in a crowded bath...'

'There's something in that,' said Dudley. 'Perhaps we should arrange a little special attention.'

'No!' cried Nan, in horror. 'No, if he's to learn it must be quietly in the holidays, somewhere else. Everything that happens to him here makes it harder.'

'Do you mean to tell the headmaster this?'

'No, I was thinking of Mrs Langton, and asking her to put it to the headmaster. I think she could make him see it.'

'Perhaps, Nan, perhaps,' said Dudley, sorrowfully. 'But do you quite like using all this diplomacy? Is it quite your style to do things in an indirect way?'

Nan hung her head, as if she had been a school-boy.

'If you don't like asking the headmaster straight out, you should think why,' Dudley continued. 'Are you really trying to do the boy a kindness, or are you just being weak?'

Nan murmured that she hardly knew.

'And our good Mrs Langton, who looks so well after our comfort—almost too well I have sometimes been ungrateful enough to think,' said Dudley. 'Is it fair to involve her in school affairs, when she so scrupulously keeps out of them?'

'Perhaps not.'

'And even if it were kind, would it be wise?' said Dudley. 'It would create a precedent. That's always a dangerous thing in a place like this. There might come a time when we were sorry to have invited her to come between the staff and the boys.'

Nan blushed.

'And the boy himself—and I ought to have put him first,' said Dudley. 'Are you sure it's in his best interests to have him let off bathing?'

46

'Absolutely sure,' said Nan. 'He'll learn nothing in the bath here.'

'Aren't you giving up hope too easily?' said Dudley. 'Aren't you going just the way to discourage the boy? Shouldn't you try to believe in him, and to bring out the best in him?'

'I don't know.'

'And Nan, it's not only the question of learning to swim; won't you make him feel isolated—one by himself? Anywhere, it's a bad thing not to be one of a group. But at school it's worse than anywhere; and so it ought to be.'

'Why?'

'Well, they're sent here to learn to mix, aren't they?'

'I suppose so,' said Nan doubtfully. 'But last year Harry wasn't allowed to bathe; he'd had bronchitis in the Lent term.'

'The boys will know the difference this time,' said Dudley. 'He's been in the bath this year.'

'Boys can be beasts,' said Nan. 'I think Harry already has rather a bad time in the Grey Room. There are very nice boys there, who are his friends, like Michael Park and Ralph Wimbush. But that horrid little Ronald Gibson plagues him, and so does George Girling.'

'Ah, Nan, there you're lumping together two very different types of boy!' said Dudley. 'Now George, he may be a bit slow, but he'll get there in the end. He's a fine chap, old George; there's really good material there, and he's as loyal as they come. D'you know, Nan, if God ever gives me a son, I would like him to be a bit like George?'

Nan blushed, aware that God must in such a case make use of some privileged woman for the accomplishment of His design.

'And he's not only the good scout that we know,' said

47

Dudley. 'There's more in George than meets the eye. Anita Rigby tells me he's a very coming artist.'

'I'm afraid he's a boy to whom I don't feel myself drawn,' said Nan, more coldly. 'Though I do dislike Ronald more.'

'That's a boy I have no use for!' said Dudley. 'I simply can't do anything with a fellow of his make up.'

'No one can make any impression on him.'

'One day I'll have to tell him what I think of him,' said Dudley grimly. 'I shall put off that day as long as I can.' (And he sounded as if he were speaking of the day of Judgement). 'It will be terrible for him, and terrible for me.'

'I'm not comfortable about Harry,' said Nan. 'There's something—I don't know what—that those two are teasing him about. Evidently he didn't want me to take it up.'

'Well, leave it for now, Nan; leave it for now,' said Dudley. 'It doesn't occur to you that it might have been something a bit discreditable to friend Staples, and that was why he wanted to keep you out of it?'

'Oh, no,' said Nan. 'I think he just didn't want anyone to get into trouble on his account.'

'Hm; that doesn't sound quite like him,' said Dudley. 'People talk a lot of rot about bullying, Nan. But boys sometimes know when they ought to take a thing into their own hands; and at a public school it's their business to do so. If a case of bullying was ever reported to me here—if I was my own master—I should be inclined to punish the boy who was bullied twice as much as the bullies.'

CHAPTER SIX

The morning hymn was heavy with foreboding.

> *At Thy feet, O Christ, we lay*
> *Thine own gift of this new day;*
> *Doubt of what it holds in store*
> *Makes us crave Thine aid the more.*

The day's work began for the sixth form with a construe lesson: the false joy of the Trojans when they thought the Greeks had gone away, and Laocoon's attack on the wooden horse. It is an exciting passage, but most of them had not managed to prepare many lines. Dudley had to fill up the hour, and felt disinclined for grammar. He gave them a little discourse on the text: *Timeo Danaos et dona ferentes.* Yes, he said, the Romans had cause to fear the gifts of the Greek world, they had indeed.

'But, sir, weren't the Greeks much more civilized?' asked Ralph. Dudley had lately told them that Athens, under Pericles, had reached 'The high-water-mark of civilization'.

Dudley said that the Greek world of the fifth century had been a very different thing; now it had only luxury and corruption to offer. It undermined the solid virtues of the Romans, which had made them a great imperial power. As an example of Roman decadence he said: 'They paid people to play games for them, instead of playing them themselves.'

'Why did they do that, sir?' said Michael Park. 'I

mean, if they didn't want to play games themselves, why bother to have games at all?'

'They liked looking on.'

'How very odd, sir!' said Ralph.

'But after all, that's what people do nowadays, sir,' said Harry. 'Aren't there professional cricketers? And didn't the headmaster have to buy tickets when he took some boys to watch county cricket last year?'

'Yes, sir,' said Michael. 'And aren't there professional footballers, who sell themselves to the League that bids highest?'

Dudley looked pained, and Ralph Wimbush plunged back mischievously into the talk: 'And then, sir, doesn't one League try to dope another League's forwards? Or is that race-horses only?'

These, said Dudley, were all dangerous symptoms of a disturbance in values that was the consequence of the war.

'Oh, sir, professional cricket is much older than that,' said Tony Stuart.

'And a very worthy profession too,' said Dudley, who added, that it was necessary to keep up the level of the game; but amateur cricket, he said, was the nation's life. Waterloo had been won on the playing-fields of Eton, and as long as people crowded to the Eton and Harrow match, so long should we have an empire on which the sun never set.

'But that's bound to end one day, sir, isn't it?' asked Harry. 'Other empires have had their day.'

There was a shocked silence.

'Has there ever been an empire quite like ours?' asked Dudley.

'I suppose no two empires have been quite alike,' said Michael.

'Well, it will last your time and mine,' said Dudley firmly. 'And I hope that of countless other generations.'

50

Then he wrote some other lines of Virgil on the board; lines that did not come in today's lesson.

Excudent alii...

He told them to leave it to foreigners to make works of art; it was the Roman task (and theirs) to give laws to the world, to spare the subject and war down the proud.

The headmaster speedily reduced two or three boys to tears. Now he came to George Girling, who had ineffectually tried to do a rider in Geometry, 'by Pythagoras', as he said.

'By Pythagoras, indeed!' snorted Mr Langton. 'And by Pythagoras, I'll touch up your hypotenuse with Twitcher before you're many hours older!'

'Twitcher' was the cane in ordinary use; there was another, 'Togo', that was darkly rumoured to have killed a boy. By other accounts, it had described a circle round him in a very extraordinary way, and had removed those parts of his body of which one did not speak, for it was a clean-mouthed school. In fact, George as well as everyone else knew the cane was an idle threat: it was never used to punish errors of the intellect, but only moral offences (Disobedience, Unpunctuality, Rudeness, Untidiness, Talking at Forbidden Times). Mistakes in one's work were not, in theory, punished except by the necessity to do it again. Nevertheless the headmaster showed his feelings.

He gripped George by the short hairs, and banged the blunt end of the pencil on his skull. Then, unthinkingly, he shifted his instrument, smashed the point on the boy's head and exclaimed in anger (he never swore).

'A little more, and he'd have driven the point into my brain!' said George in a shocked voice.

'If you had a brain,' said Michael. 'You don't have to worry.'

51

'The man makes my blood boil!' said George.

'Well, you can cool it in the swimming-bath,' said someone.

The dank green pool was again awaiting them. A leaf or two floated on the surface, and a grey cloud screened it from the sun.

All the better, said Matron, there was less danger of sunstroke; but they must duck their heads all the same, to be on the safe side. George Girling again plunged in, and hit the water with a resounding smack.

Kit watched with pity—and with exasperation at their fate—the nonswimmers holding on at the shallow end; they looked like an illustration to Dante. They were waiting for his signal of release, and he gave it half a minute early.

At this moment the headmaster appeared.

'Harry Staples,' he called. 'Didn't I tell you to remind me to put you in the belt today?'

'Mr Henderson's just blown the whistle, sir,' said Harry, shivering on the brink.

'All the better; you'll have the bath to yourself,' said Mr Langton. 'Put that towel away, and come here.'

Harry's lips turned blue.

'He's saying his prayers!' said Ronald, and so he was. 'St Patrick's Breastplate' covers most of the principal dangers of school-life.

> *Against all Satan's spells and wiles,*
> *Against false words of heresy,*
> *Against the knowledge that defiles,*
> *Against the heart's idolatry,*
> *Against the wizard's evil craft,*
> *Against the death-wound, and the burning,*
> *The choking wave, the poisoned shaft—*
> *Protect me, Christ, till Thy returning.*

Mr Langton slipped the canvas belt over Harry's head, and tightened it round the waist; then he gripped the pole.

Harry moved towards the shallow end.

'No, we'll have you in at the deep end,' said Mr Langton.

He dragged him along the side of the bath, where quiet cows munched the grass on the other side of the fence.

'Oh, sir, please, not!' cried out Harry.

'In you go!' cried Mr Langton, and gave him a push.

At first, after the drop, Harry's mouth was too full of water for more than a feeble splutter. He grasped the edge of the bath and, as his breath came back to him, gave scream after scream.

'No, you don't do that,' said the headmaster, kicking his hands off the edge. 'Just relax, take it easy, and make the strokes. You make them well enough on dry land.'

Harry made an effort to cleave the water with his arms, but he tried to raise his head high out of it. His body sagged, and he went under again. When he came up, he cried: 'I can't!'

'Oh, you can't, can't you?' cried the headmaster, banging his body against the side. 'Well, we'll do this every day till you can, d'you hear?'

By this time he had completely lost patience, and took no more trouble to teach than Harry to learn. He quickly dragged the belt the length of the bath to the shallow end, without caring if the boy put out a hand to the side, or stumbled with his feet on the bottom. Harry, whose nerve was quite broken, never stopped screaming.

Mr Langton released him, gave him a parting prod in the buttock with the pole, and a flick on the shoulder with the canvas belt.

'Cut along!' he said. 'I hope you're pleased with yourself. Son of a colonel, too!'

Kit and Matron, by walking in front of the shed, and hustling the boys, had prevented most of them from taking in the full horror of the scene. Matron now enfolded the skinny, shivering body with a towel, and imprinted a kiss on the wet hair.

Kit walked up to the house with him.

'You must try not to let this upset you too much, Harry,' he said.

'But it's going to happen every day,' said Harry hopelessly.

'Indeed it's not!' said Kit, who did not intend to remain at the school another day, unless he were sure of this. 'I shall speak to my uncle and aunt; I promise you it won't happen again.'

'Thank you, sir.'

'You must try to forgive my uncle, Harry,' said Kit. 'I suppose he wanted to assure himself that you couldn't learn that way; he'll give up now.'

Harry murmured assent; and yet he did not seem to like the idea that he had been given up as a bad job.

'That's the sort of idea a woman must have put into your head!' said Kit with disgust. 'And I bet it wasn't Matron.'

Harry, however, was wondering what would become of him when he went to his public school.

'They can't do worse!' said Kit. 'They can't drown you. I should get your parents or someone to write and have you let off bathing. That oughtn't to be too difficult to arrange. Why bother whether you can swim or not? It's a very over-rated pleasure. I don't think it's much fun in fresh water, or in the English climate.'

'But isn't it the best climate, sir?'

'It depends what for— I daresay it is for gooseberries. It's certainly not the best for swimming. I only care about it in the Mediterranean, in warm, salt water. You'd probably like it then.'

'I'd still be a funk, sir,' said Harry despondently.

'I don't think you are,' said Kit. 'Though I can see why you think you are. I'm afraid people have told you that's what you are.'

'Everyone here has, sir.'

'You exaggerate, Harry,' said Kit. 'Quite a lot of boys haven't; and I haven't, and Matron certainly hasn't. She told me you were quite fearless at the dentist's, while that Girling creature blubbed like anything.'

'One has to go through with it, sir,' said Harry. 'What's the point of making a fuss?'

'It's you who are right,' said Kit. 'But some people aren't so stoical. D'you know, being cold and being frightened are much the same thing—Matron tells me that you have a bad circulation, and have chilblains in the winter. You'll never learn to swim in cold fresh water; much better give up the attempt. Once you've learned in warm, salt water, then you can swim anywhere—if you want to.'

'This mustn't happen again, Aunt Mary,' said Kit.

'Of course not, Christopher; your uncle knows this as well as you or I. His bark is worse than his bite.'

'I gave Harry my word.'

'You were quite safe to do so, Christopher.'

'Poor boy, at such an unattractive stage in his development!' said Kit. 'He's let them persuade him that he's a funk—and someone (or several people) are doing their best to make him a little prig. He oughtn't to be either—he's got the best mind in the school, after Michael Park.'

'Don't tell your uncle I said so,' said Mary. 'I'm afraid school can only make him worse. One must just hope that its effects aren't indelible.'

'He needs his mother.'

'And to all intents and purposes he hasn't got one, poor child,' said Mary. 'She ran away.'

'Abominably cruel of her,' said Kit.

'Oh, Christopher, I don't feel I can judge her,' said Mary. 'She didn't go off with a lover, you see; she just had to get away. Poor little Harry wouldn't be much of a bond, do you think, if he was all one had in common with a man one hated.'

'But he must need his mother more than most other children would.'

'What we mean is, I'm afraid—because one has come to dislike the word so much—that he needs love,' said Mary.

'Then that means he needs his mother,' said Kit. 'No one else would be likely to find him very lovable at his present stage.'

'So you think it's a vicious circle?' said Mary. 'I'm not so sure, Christopher. After one's earliest infancy (perhaps) for some of us, it doesn't so very much matter if we are loved. What we need is someone or something to love.'

'And I gather Dudley thinks you know nothing about boys!'

'I don't see a lot of the boys,' said Mary. 'And Dudley reasons from that. You know how stupidly people reason that way—"What", they say, "can Professor X. know about life?"'

'And what can they know about what he knows?' said Kit. 'People are always ready to think that other people's experience is limited; they never remember the limitations of their own minds and imaginations.'

'I've lived fifty-odd years, and I've picked up a few things about people,' said Mary. 'And boys are people after all.'

'That's more than Dudley will ever know,' said Kit.

'Any way, you and Matron may be just enough to make Harry's life worth living,' said Mary. 'The young don't ask much—and I don't mean that you and Matron are not much to him.'

'D'you know, he bears no malice against Uncle Dick?'

'I'm not surprised. Your uncle is Jehovah. He's like a force of nature. Boys don't love or hate him.'

'Dudley excites stronger feelings I believe, in either direction.'

'Yes,' said Mary. 'He's not Old Testament but New, and not Authorized but Revised. Don't ask me who he is, because it is really horribly shocking, and I don't want to blaspheme.'

'"The Imitation of Christ",' said Kit.

'You put it as gently as one can,' said Mary. 'But what an imitation! How blasphemous and horrible! Have you watched him yearning over the boys, or looking on them sorrowfully....'

'"And the eyes of Dudley still ask questions of the soul",' murmured Kit.

CHAPTER SEVEN

Michael Park flung three mugfuls of milk out of the window.

'Gosh, I nearly let one mug go!' he said.

Elated at the narrow avoidance of danger, he leapt out of bed the moment the bell rang, tore off his pyjamas, and pirouetted in the middle of the Grey Room.

'You'll be swished if you're found naked like that,' said George Girling.

'Brethren,' said Michael, in a solemn voice, 'I'm going to found a new Purity League. Any takers? Members must never, at any moment, wear less than three garments.' He slipped a garter over each arm, and hung a tie round his neck.

Harry followed suit with one sock, and a pair of braces. 'One says "a pair of braces", so I count it as two garments,' he said.

Ralph tied a tie round his hair, and pushed a hand into either bed-room slipper.

'Absurd nonsense!' said George Girling.

'Oh, throw a jerry at Girlie, Tony or someone.'

Tony took his chamberpot by the handle, made a dangerous gesture with it, and indeed spilt a drop or two.

'Disgusting!' said George. 'What would you have said if you'd spilt the lot?'

'Please Matron, I've had rather a nasty accident,' chanted Tony in monotone, and then he sang out clearly: 'And I upset my po!'

'We'd better leave chambering and wantonness,' said Michael, aware that authority would come down most heavily upon him, if they were caught at their pranks.

'What would they call it in the "Black Book"?' asked Harry. 'There isn't a column for "chambering and wantonness".'

' "Rudeness", I daresay,' said Michael. 'That covers a multitude of sins.'

At Prayers Mr Langton read them a very nice passage from the Pentateuch, which was restfully remote from anything that could possibly concern them. Mr Knight —for it was Empire Day—gave thanks for the Empire and all its benefits, and prayed for its continuance. With noticeably less confidence he prayed that those present might show themselves worthy of this goodly heritage; it almost sounded as if he thought he were asking something unreasonably difficult of the Almighty. He wound up his petitions with a request that they might not accept a life of ease, while others toiled for their comfort.

Mrs Langton struck a chord, and they sang:

> *We are but little children meek,*
> *Nor born to any high estate...*

'Who does Dudley think is going to toil for their comfort?' asked Kit. 'Is this such a grand school, that any proportion of them will be able to live a life of ease?'

'I'm afraid not many of them will have the chance,' said Mary. 'And it sounds such heaven, doesn't it?'

'You answered him back splendidly with that hymn.'

'I'm afraid I was forgetting the little Pilkington boy,' said Mary. 'His mother did once ask me to take special care of him, because he might possibly come in for an earldom one day.'

'And what special care did you take?'

59

'I put him on the list of boys to be called with milk in the morning,' said Mary. 'That's all I could think of.'

'Poor little chap!'

'Oh, I expect he chucks it away like the rest of them,' said Mary.

Kit took the sixth form for French. For a change he let Ralph Wimbush conduct the conversation.

'*Que font les jeunes gens à cette école, Michel?*'

'They do their lessons, and their problems of arithmetic.'

'What does Matron do?'

'She gives the boys aspirin, and superintends their baths.'

'A good idea, Rodolphe, go on,' said Kit.

'What does Miss Rigby do, Henry?'

'As you can hear, she teaches music!' And not far off she was putting a boy through his harmonic scales.

'*Et les Beaux Arts,*' added Ralph; for small boys did Art, and so did sixth form dunces, who did not do Greek. George Girling was even rather good at it in a nasty slick way.

'What does the headmaster do, Guy?'

'He administers corporal punishment, when necessary.'

There was laughter.

'*Que fait le Révérend Père le Chevalier?*' asked Ralph.

'*Mais non, Rodolphe, vous exagérez!*' said Kit, and the question was framed more suitably. Mr Knight was said to teach Latin and to read prayers in the morning and evening.

'I wanted to give you a poem to learn,' said Kit. 'But all the stuff in your book is such rubbish.'

'Why not dictate something, sir?' said Michael. 'Mr MacLeod does in English.'

'All right,' said Kit, opening a book he had brought in with him; he turned over some of it. 'This might do,' he said, and they wrote out a bit of *Gastibelza*.

> *Vraiment la reine eût près d'elle été laide*
> *Quand, vers le soir,*
> *Elle passait sur le pont de Tolède*
> *En corset noir.*
> *Un chapelet du temps de Charlemagne*
> *Ornait son cou—*
> *Le vent qui vient à travers la montagne*
> *Me rendra fou!*

He could see, of course, that for one or two of them Tony Stuart, who was scratching rather irritatingly with his pen, was 'Sabine'— and that they thought Spain and Peru would be well thrown away for a look from him. But you can't (he thought) stop Music because for some people it may be the food of love—at least, if you don't provide good Music, love will only make its food off bad. Any way, the lines might stay in their heads, even if Tony broke his nose or erupted into spots; and they might hang Charlemagne's jewel round other throats. Anyhow, some of them just enjoyed the sound, while for most of them it was just 'French'; for himself it was a method of improving their accents.

In break they went to put on their scout uniforms, and the last morning hour was occupied by a parade. This was held on the sunk lawn, under the beech tree. A few benches were brought out to accommodate the staff, and those boys who were not yet scouts.

Dudley, in scout's uniform, directed proceedings. Miss Rigby had had a Girl Guide's uniform run up for her by her dress-maker, with one or two individual touches. She was there to conduct the singing, which began with *Land of Hope and Glory*.

'Dudley looks every inch a clergyman, doesn't he?' said Mary.

'All the more, with those bare knees,' whispered Kit.

Dudley gave various orders about staves, and at length the scouts stood at ease to listen to him.

He told them that most of them had already taken the most solemn possible oath. A few more were to take it today—if they had any hesitation, or any doubt about their power to keep this oath, it was still in their power to withdraw. They had sworn to do their duty to God and the King, to help other people at all times, and to obey the Scout Law. Of course, by their baptism, they were bound to do their duty to God; and as his subjects, they were bound to honour and obey the King. But the scout-promise joined them together with scouts of all colours who, in a special way, were bound in loyalty to the King-Emperor, in every part of that empire on which the sun never set. Yes, in spite of downhearted people, he would say that empire on which the sun would never set.

He then told them of their great example, the Prince of Wales, that messenger of friendship and good will throughout the English speaking world.

He rehearsed some of the articles of the scout law.

' "Lord have mercy upon us, and incline our hearts to keep this law!" ' murmured Kit irreverently.

'The scout smiles and whistles under all difficulties,' said Dudley.

'How maddening that must be!' whispered Mary Langton.

'The scout is a friend to all, and a brother to every other scout—no matter to what social class the other belongs.'

'Even if he's a duke?' murmured Kit. 'Rather presumptuous, I should say.'

'I don't suppose Sir Robert Baden-Powell thought of

that,' said Mary. 'I think he meant that we were to be condescending to the lower orders. We only talk about class when we're thinking of our social inferiors.'

Miss Hackett gave them a pained look.

Friendship, said Dudley, that was really the ideal of scouting, put in one word. He ended by saying that the scout must be pure in thought, word and deed; and he grimly implied that with every day that must become more difficult.

One by one the new scouts of the year advanced, saluted Dudley, repeated the promise, and received a handshake.

Ronald Gibson, who had for some reason missed last year's investiture, came forward, and took the oath.

'I promise on my honour to do my best to do my duty to God and the King, to help other people at all times, and to obey the scout law.'

There was a general and audible intake of breath.

'And I trust you, on your honour, to keep that promise,' said Dudley, shaking his hand, and looking sorrowfully upon him.

They sang: *God save the King*.

'That wasn't a nice ceremony,' said Kit. 'So totemistic.'

'And that wretched Gibson boy,' said Mary. 'It reminded me of something at the time, but I can't remember what.'

'It made me think of French history,' said Kit. 'All those wicked people whom Louis XIV forced to receive the sacraments in public. There must have been the same intake of breath.'

'Fortunately there's no sacrilege involved this time,' said Mary. 'Though I'm afraid Dudley did his best to make the boys think so.'

'"Mother of the free", indeed!' said Kit. 'What

63

heroism a boy would have needed, if he'd decided not to make the promise!'

'I shouldn't like to see such a brave action,' said Mary. 'I think it would make me cry—and anyhow it would give me far too high a standard forever afterwards. I'm glad Ronald went through with it; I see his father has come to take him home to luncheon, as it's a half-holiday.'

A group of boys were left standing with Matron; it was still early for school dinner.'

'Ronald's gone off home,' said Tony. 'Very wise, I think.'

'He looked as if he thought the earth would swallow him, when he was being sworn in,' said Ralph.

'Why does Mr Knight bother to take a promise from someone like that?' said Harry. 'He must know it's worth nothing.'

'Oh, you shouldn't talk like that,' said Matron. 'It isn't kind.'

'Mr Knight is giving him his chance,' said George. 'I don't think he'd break such a solemn promise.'

'He only promised to do his best,' said Ralph. 'That isn't much in his case.'

'He didn't make any promise,' said Michael. 'He promised on his honour—and he hasn't got any.'

Several boys laughed.

'Now that's too bad,' said Matron.

'His father's a fine chap,' said George.

'We know he plays golf with the headmaster,' said Michael. 'So I suppose he's quite good at that. What else is fine about him?'

'Ronald took me home one Sunday,' began George.

'Couldn't get anyone else to go,' said someone. 'And he wouldn't like to tell his people that he hadn't any friends.'

'And George would go anywhere for food,' said Hugh.

64

'Well, I hope it was good,' said Ralph.

'I've eaten their salt,' began George pompously.

'Dear! Where does he get hold of these expressions?' said Matron with admiration.

'From Mr Knight, I should think,' said Michael. 'I hope they gave you something else besides salt, George?'

'It's rude to ask people what they had, when they've been to a meal in someone else's house,' said Matron.

'I know it is,' said Ralph. 'But one does like to know.'

'What does the family consist of?' asked Matron.

There was the Colonel, it appeared, and his rather military sister. Between them they ruled the roost, and Mrs Gibson did not count for much. There was also a dotty old grandmother who kept confusing people in her memory, and for a time she took George for her grandson. You couldn't help laughing (said George).

'The Colonel and his sister ragged her terrifically,' he added. 'They told her I was Ronald, and that she must congratulate me on getting a prize for Trigonometry. Of course she didn't know what it was, and couldn't say the word.'

'Do you know what it is?' asked Michael.

'I think it was disgusting of them,' said Harry. 'I think they sound the most horrible people I've ever heard of.'

'She didn't understand,' said George.

'It's one thing to laugh kindly at her muddles,' said Harry. 'Quite another to draw the poor old woman out, and to make fun of her to amuse a guest.'

'I do so agree,' said Matron warmly.

'They sound exactly the sort of people you'd expect Ronald to have,' said Michael. ' "A tree is known by its fruit".'

'He's not his aunt's fruit,' said Hugh.

'My mother talked to Mrs Gibson last sports' day,'

65

said Ralph. 'She told me she was a nasty, spiteful, little woman and (she thought) a great liar.'

'We're criticizing a boy's parents,' said George, sticking—as it was only too easy to do—his nose in the air.

'He's not here,' said Tony.

'Shows what funks you are,' said George. 'You wouldn't dare do it if he were here.'

'Nobody is afraid of Ronald,' said Hugh.

'It shows we have ordinary good manners and good feeling,' said Ralph.

'We're not criticizing the Gibsons,' said Michael. 'We've decided they're beneath our criticism.'

'I should be a little careful my dears,' said Matron. 'Sometimes things get repeated, and do harm. I think George is right to stick up for people who have been kind to him, though I'm not sure that they're very nice friends to have.'

'Most families have their skeletons,' said Michael. 'But they do try to keep them in the cupboard.'

'Well, what about you, Ralph?' said George. 'Didn't you say your mother was in seduced circumstances?'

Ralph burst out laughing.

'My dear, I'm sure he never said anything like that,' said Matron. 'You must never say that again, George.'

'Dear Mama will dine out on that for a month, as she would say,' said Ralph.

'You won't tell her?' said George, reddening to the tip of his nose.

'I couldn't keep it from her; it would be too unkind,' said Ralph. 'As she's in reduced circumstances, she can't afford not to dine out on you.'

'Dear, dear! Some of you boys are too grownup for your age,' said Matron.

CHAPTER EIGHT

'I'd like to have a talk with your young nephew, Langton,' said Dudley. 'You have no objection?'

'What's he been up to?' asked the headmaster.

'I'm sure nothing he shouldn't,' said his wife.

'He's a good lad,' said Dick Langton. 'His mother is my favourite sister. It was very good of him to come and help us out like this, when poor Fanshawe let us down suddenly.'

'He's been a brick!' said Dudley. 'He's a fine young fellow.'

'Then I hope you're not going to upset him, Mr Knight,' said Mary.

'Now, why should I want to upset him?' asked Dudley, with a broad smile. 'I just feel, here's a young fellow with all his life before him—perhaps he'd like the chance of a heart-to-heart talk with an older man who can help him to see one or two things more clearly.'

'He's in his uncle's house,' said Mary.

'Oh, I don't want to butt in,' said Dudley, with a humble little laugh that ended in a giggle. 'But one is a sky-pilot....'

'I think there must be something special that you want to talk to Christopher about,' said Mary. 'Would you care to tell us?'

'Well, now you are helping me, Mrs Langton, as I was sure you would,' said Dudley. 'What I'm thinking of is his reading.'

'I only hope he has enough time for it,' said Langton.

'That is one of the sacrifices that he's making for us. The months between school and the university are important months for reading—Kit is quite a well-read boy; but a man's standard of reading is another thing. He's got to deepen his knowledge all round—and then he needs to read the books of the day. When he goes up to Cambridge he'll hear them discussed.'

'Now that's the point, Langton: the books of the day,' said Dudley. 'I confess I haven't a lot of sympathy with them. Hugh Walpole is a fine writer, of course; his work will live. But I saw a book lying in the staff-room the other day, and it had young Henderson's name in it...'

'Nothing improper, I hope?' put in Mary.

'No, no!' said Dudley, blushing. 'It was a modern work of biography. The author seemed determined to denigrate the people about whom he was writing. The book seemed to me—from the little I read of it—filled with the spirit that denies...'

'I didn't think the Church of England put books on the Index,' said Mary.

'Heaven forbid!' said Dudley, striking the arm of a chair with his hand. 'Every man should be free to read what his conscience allows him. But some books are dangerous, and a little advice may not come amiss.'

'I should never presume to direct the reading of a clever young man of Christopher's age,' said Mary.

'Oh, dear!' said Dudley, raising both hands in humorous protest, 'I'm afraid we're talking at cross purposes. I'd never try to direct him. He's later from school; I hope he may put me on to a good book or two—little time though I have for reading. I only felt I should like to talk to Christopher; may I call him so...?'

'I'm sure I don't know,' said Mary.

'Call him so to you, I mean,' said Dudley, taking the permission as granted. 'To talk over this book—and other books—with Christopher. I've no doubt he ought at least to glance at books he'll hear talked about—but couldn't he do with a little help in this, and perhaps other things?'

'I don't know,' said Dick Langton. 'You'd better ask him.'

'Thank you,' said Dudley. 'I didn't want to say anything out of order, or to trespass on your privileges. But after all, I do wear my collar back to front....'

'That must protect him from hearing what people think of his impertinence,' said Mary, as the door closed behind him. 'Though I don't see why a woman and a clergyman shouldn't have a good slanging-match, as it's supposed to be cowardly in other people to insult either of them.'

'I hope you won't,' said Dick Langton.

'So silly, really,' continued Mary. 'Positively anachronistic. As if anyone else was liable to draw a sword on you or to call you out! They could only use their tongues; and women and clergymen are rather good with those.'

'The man means well,' said Langton lazily.

'My dear, have you ever met anyone who didn't mean well; with the possible exception of the boy Ronald Gibson?' asked Mary.

'Will you take a little turn with me on the terrace?' asked Dudley.

'With pleasure, sir,' said Kit.

'Ah—Christopher—if I may? You don't have to call me "sir".'

'Very well.'

'I was saying to your good uncle and aunt that I wanted to have a word with you,' said Dudley. 'I wouldn't like you to feel that I was infringing upon their rights in any way.'

'Oh, no; of course not,' said Kit vaguely.

69

'My dear boy,' said Dudley gripping his arm. 'I know you do a lot of reading.'

'I try to do what I can,' said Kit. 'I've brought a good many books of my own, and I've invested in a Times Library Subscription.'

'A wonderful thing to have time for reading!' sighed Dudley. 'I saw a biographical book belonging to you in the staff-room the other day. Do you care for that kind of book?'

'I can't for the moment think of other books of the kind,' said Kit. 'But yes; I found that one very amusing.'

'Too amusing, I'm afraid,' said Dudley. 'I took the liberty of reading a few pages, and I felt I disliked the man very much: he takes great men and women and puts them in the pillory in order to crack a few sophisticated jokes....'

'I'm not quite sure how accurate he is,' said Kit. 'A history master at Ragstead told me to take him with a pinch of salt. But it's a lively book; and I think one doesn't dislike his principal characters after one has read it. I think they seem more human, and one likes them more.'

'Don't you feel a lack of reverence?' asked Dudley.

'Well, sir—I beg your pardon; wash out the "sir"! It's your job not mine; you're the parson. But ought we to have reverence except for God and sacred things?'

'Ah, Christopher, but aren't great men and women, and the inspiration that their memory has been to those who come after—aren't they sacred?'

'Not unless they were saints, I should have thought.'

'Ah, but what makes the saint?' said Dudley. 'It isn't a place in the calendar, or a stained glass window showing someone with a halo, and a face longer than God gave him. There are many unobtrusive humble people that are true saints of God.'

'I'm sure,' said Kit. 'I've been living in Roman

Catholic countries lately, you know. I understand the Church doesn't make saints, but tells us whom we are to reverence as saints.'

'Do we need telling?'

'I should have thought so,' said Kit. 'Of course each of us may respect someone in whom he sees special goodness and beauty of character; as I've seen it in someone here, I think.'

Dudley began to purr.

'In Matron, I mean,' said Kit. 'But I wouldn't have any right to expect other people, who've never known her, to accept her as a saint except on better authority than mine.'

'Hm, perhaps,' said Dudley, rather as if he had expected a different candidate for canonization to be proposed. 'Well, even if we use different words sometimes, I'm sure you're sound, Christopher. I'm sure you wouldn't let a cynical, sophisticated writer upset your faith in fundamentals, in all the standards you learned at your great school. I know the modern generation tends to question these things....'

'I think every generation has to question things,' said Christopher. 'They always have, haven't they?'

'I'm not for a man refusing to use the brains God gave him,' said Dudley. 'You don't suppose I didn't have a tussle with Doubt, before I could make up my mind to put on my collar the way you see me wear it?'

'I'm sure,' said Kit civilly.

'But your generation seems to stand at a parting of the ways; and it's up to each of you to choose the right way,' said Dudley. 'I think it's a particularly difficult time to be young.'

'I don't suppose it's ever easy,' said Kit.

Dudley tightened the grip on his arm. 'Ah, I know, dear boy,' he murmured. 'All the difficulties of a strong young body, which is continually making more and

71

more imperious demands that cannot yet honourably be satisfied. If you ever want to talk things over, I should like you to feel that I am very much at your service.'

'Thank you very much,' said Kit, freeing his arm, and putting it behind his back, so that it could not easily be held again.

'I know you have your good uncle, but sometimes it isn't to one's family that one wants to turn,' said Dudley.

Kit turned to his aunt as soon as he possibly could.

'I've had a pi-jaw from Dudley,' he said. 'At least that's what we should have called it at school. I feel wobbly.'

'I think he'd call it a heart-to-heart talk,' said Mary.

'He did nearly all the talking,' said Kit. 'But it was a strain.'

'I can imagine it.'

'He wanted to assure himself that I was "sound", in spite of a little modern reading. Would he be afraid that I was going to corrupt the boys with nasty French novels?'

'No, I think he knows they are only in the *bijou, caillou, chou, genou* stage,' said Mary. 'I think it was all for your own good—your "real good", as he would say.'

'Hereafter?' asked Kit.

'Oh, no; "here and now",' said Mary.

'How very impertinent!'

'I shall get you a drink, Christopher, you need one,' said Mary.

'Thank you!' said Kit. 'I shouldn't have liked to cadge one from MacLeod.'

'I doubt if anyone could,' said Mary. 'Any way, he's out tonight, celebrating empire, I suppose.'

'I wonder what his trouble is?' said Kit. 'There must be one.'

'I think Dudley tried to find out; but he was sent

away pretty quickly with a flea in his ear. I expect he thought it was sex.'

'He would!' said Kit. 'If it was, MacLeod must pretty well have solved that problem—but a crude solution. What do the boys think about him?'

'They've never seen him other than sober,' said Mary. 'Did Dudley try to talk to you about sex?'

'Did he not!' said Kit. 'He asked me not to hesitate to bring my troubles to him, if I had any.'

'Not very nice,' said Mary, with distaste. 'Oh, dear! What's that noise?'

It was MacLeod, in an advanced state of drink, thundering on the door.

'Open, I shay! Open in the name of the Lorrd! I'm Christ Almighty, and I'll burrn ye all up....'

'We'll have to get your uncle, and he'll get the gardener,' said Mary.

'I hope the boys won't hear.'

'Something for them to write in their letters home,' said Mary.

Fortunately MacLeod soon passed into unconsciousness, and the headmaster and the gardener carried him up to his room, removed his boots, and locked him in.

'A terrible thing, drink!' said Dudley, looking malevolently at Kit's and Mary's glasses.

'Yes,' said Mary. 'Have some, Mr Knight? We all need it.'

'No, no; you know my view,' said Dudley, 'I think we ought to abstain for the sake of the weaker brethren.'

'Every man has a right to his opinion,' said the headmaster, helping himself. 'No harm in abstinence, so long as you don't force it on other people. "Better England free than England sober."'

'"Mother of the sober",' said Mary. 'That wouldn't sound well in the song, would it? And no possible rhyme except October, and *Das geht nicht!*'

73

Dudley's indignation issued in a strange hissing sound.

'We'll get MacLeod out of the way tomorrow,' said Dick Langton. 'We'll tell the boys he had a breakdown—which is perfectly true. Luckily he only taught English subjects; we can all do his work between us. Nan and Miss Rigby can help us out too.'

CHAPTER NINE

Some of the boys stood in the play-room window, watching the first eleven climb into a brake to go and play a match against Hazelford.

'There's Tony,' said Michael.

'And Guy helping him in,' said Ralph.

'Miss Rigby seems to be going with them,' said Harry. 'I suppose we can't spare a master, now MacLeod is in a drunkards' home.'

'We ought to try to conceal that from other schools,' said Ralph.

'Miss Rigby always goes with the Eleven to Hazelford,' said Michael. 'She's got a sister on the staff there. The sister comes here when they come to play us at Hazelcroft.'

'Awkward for them, being on different sides,' said George.

'You really are more of a little boy than one would have thought possible!' said Ralph. 'Do you really imagine grownup people care what happens in a cricket match?'

'I should hope the staff did,' said George, sticking up his nose.

'Of course our Miss Rigby would prefer us to do well,' said Harry. 'There's Dick's temper to be considered.'

'I hope she'd be above thinking of that first.'

'I'm not,' said Ralph.

'Nor am I,' said Michael and Harry.

'I expect the two sisters have other things to talk about,' said Michael. 'I bet they don't watch the match. They go to a tea-shop and eat jam tarts, and talk about how beastly their headmasters are.'

'This time there's all the MacLeod story,' added Ralph.

'"Ah've come in powerr and great glorry",' quoted someone; for the story had received some embellishments.

'I hope Deadly Nightshade is going with the Eleven,' said Michael.

'You bet Miss Rigby hopes it too!' said Ralph. '"Dudley the cuddly"—what a revolting idea!'

'No, Kit Henderson is getting in,' said Harry. 'What a shame! I'd much rather have him on duty here.'

'He won't be much good to Miss Rigby,' said Ralph. 'But it's an ill wind that blows no woman good—think how pleased Nan must be!'

'And I'm pleased,' said George. 'Good old Dud!'

Cricket was left more or less to itself, as the Eleven was absent. Matron was at hand, in case any bruises called for witch hazel.

Those who were not fielding roamed about as they wished at the edge of the field. It was a favourite occupation to hunt for four-leaved clover, which brings luck, and may be hoped to avert some of the misfortunes likely to attend on school life. The smaller boys were fond of gathering posies of vetch, ragged robin, Queen Anne's lace and quaker grass; these were brought as offerings to Matron, or to Mrs Langton, if ever she appeared.

'So boring to have wilting wild flowers in one's room!' said Mary more than once. 'I wish one could have a shrine at a Church of England school; but I suppose Mr Knight wouldn't like it. Perhaps a pets'

76

cemetery would be the thing? They need somewhere to put those wispy objects.'

Harry greeted Michael, who was sprawled under a beech tree:

'*Tityre, tu patulae recubans sub tegmine fagi...*'

They had done some of the Eclogues last term, and Michael replied:

'*O Meliboee, deus nobis haec otia fecit* ... How I adore cricket, when one hasn't anything to do!'

Ralph came up, plucking at a daisy.

'Who loves you, or loves you not?' asked Michael lazily. 'And who cares?'

'I'm not playing it for myself,' said Ralph, 'I'm playing it for Nan. "He loves her, he loves her not."' He threw himself down on the grass. 'It seems he loves her not,' he concluded.

'I'll do it for Miss Rigby,' said Michael. '"He loves her, he loves her not". D'you know, he doesn't love her either?'

'I'm not surprised,' said Ralph, closing his eyes.

Harry lay back and watched for dragonflies; here they were abundant, and most beautiful, with great blue or reddish-brown wings.

'Where's George?' said Michael.

'Does it matter?' said Ralph. 'I rather think he's pretending to take an interest in the game; so as to please the Master if he cometh.'

'Silly ass,' said Michael. 'It's much more fun being foolish virgins like us.'

'George doesn't care any more about the game than we do,' said Harry.

'I daresay he cares ten times as much as I do,' said Michael. 'Ten times nought is nought.'

'You fellows look as if no one had hired you,' said Dudley, suddenly appearing in the midst of them. 'Anyone who cares for an extra bathe, come on!'

Michael and Ralph went after him, and a few other boys were picked up on the way.

George Girling came up to Harry, as he was walking back to the house at the end of play.

'Where are Park and Wimbush?' he asked.

'Michael and Ralph?' said Harry. 'Oh, Deadly Nightshade came down to the field, and took them off for a bathe.'

'What?'

'Oh, he suggested an extra bathe for anyone who wanted.'

'And I didn't know!' said George, and burst into tears.

'It's nothing to blub about,' said Harry.

'But I've missed a bathe!' sobbed George. 'The Dud might have told me! One of you might have told me.'

'I suppose no one saw you about.'

'Why didn't you go?' asked George accusingly, as he dried his eyes.

'It wasn't compulsory.'

'Don't you do anything you don't have to do?'

'Not bathing,' said Harry firmly.

'A good chance for you, when the bath is empty,' said George. 'You might learn to swim. The Dud wouldn't scare you like Dick.'

'Kit Henderson says I'll never learn here,' said Harry. 'He thinks I might learn quickly in warm salt water, in the Mediterranean.'

'Fat lot of use, as you don't live there,' said George.

'One might go in the holidays,' said Harry.

'You missed a lovely bathe,' said Ronald, as they were going to bed.

'I don't know why I wasn't told about it,' said George haughtily.

'Oh, it was just a thing decided on the spur of the

78

moment,' said Michael. 'Deadly Nightshade just told anyone he happened to see.'

'He told Harry; and he didn't go.'

'That was Harry's business,' said Michael. 'He'd have told him to go, if he meant him to.'

'Perhaps not, as it was something extra,' said George.

'You mean, he'd have no right to order him to go, if he didn't want to?' said Michael. 'Then it's all the more Harry's business.'

'Of course, if he won't take his chance of learning to swim, before he goes to a public school,' began George.

'I'm a bit tired of hearing about public schools,' said Ralph. 'One isn't there for life, you know. It's a thing to go through for the sake of one's education. It needn't be so bad.'

'Mr Henderson says I may find my own niche at Slowborough,' quoted Harry.

'Not if it's like any school I've ever heard of,' said George.

'My dear George, your reading is confined to *Chums* and *The Boys' Own Paper*,' said Michael wearily. 'There's a lot you don't know. You only know about bad boys drinking in pubs, and smoking on the roof. The real books about public schools wouldn't be allowed in our library.'

'I found one at home,' said Ralph. 'Someone had lent it to Mother. She snatched it away from me pretty quickly.'

'Kit Henderson says that any good public school must have its points,' said Harry. 'He says there are bound to be a few really first-rate men teaching the sixth, and that that does make a difference.'

'Well, haven't we got first-rate men here?' said George indignantly. 'I don't mean Kit—he's only a big boy—but Mr Langton?'

'Kit said how good Mr Langton was,' said Harry. 'But

he hasn't had the training a sixth form master would have to have had—he didn't need it.'

'And what about the Dud?'

'Henderson didn't go on with the subject,' said Harry.

'He'd give Deadly Nightshade Benefit of Clergy,' said Ralph.

'You don't mean the Dud's not first-rate?' said George, thrusting his nose threateningly into Ralph's face.

'I've looked him up in the Clerical Register,' said Michael. 'He got a third class degree—he's third-rate.'

'You don't expect much at prep schools,' said Ralph. 'Where else would a soak like MacLeod get a job?'

'Henderson is much the best,' said Michael. 'He's only here to help out. Once he's been through Cambridge they won't get him again.'

'I don't think so much of Kit Henderson,' said George. 'He ought to be still at school. He would be, if he was a real success there.'

'He was a success,' said Michael. 'He got a Cambridge scholarship just before Christmas. What on earth was there to stay on for?'

'He missed his last two terms at school,' said George. 'He wouldn't do that if he was a real blood. They must be the best of all, if you're Head of the School or Captain of Cricket—particularly if you've no work to do.'

'There's no point in being at school if one's no work to do,' said Harry. 'One goes there to work, not to swank.'

'I daresay he wasn't anything like that,' said Michael. 'And if he was, it probably seemed rather schoolboyish to him. When you're practically grownup, you can't really care about all those scarves and ties—and so hideous they usually are too.'

'To be a tin-pot hero at school!' said Ralph. 'When one could travel, and see Italy!'

'England's good enough for me!' said George.

'You'd better make the most of your public school, if you pass into one, which I doubt,' said Ralph. 'They get rid of dunces rather quickly; it's called "superannuation".'

'"The very word is beautiful!"' quoted Michael, who had heard that the Greeks said that of democracy.

'Kit Henderson was obviously a terrific brain,' said Ralph. 'I don't think he was specially good at games and all that.'

'Then he can't have been a real success at Ragstead,' said George.

'Nonsense,' said Ralph. 'There are a lot of different ways of succeeding at school.'

'It's said to be the world in miniature,' said Tony Stuart.

'Rot, Tony,' said Michael.

'The Dud said so in a sermon.'

'Sort of thing he would say!' said Michael. 'But if you think twice, you see it's not true.'

'D'you call him a liar?' said George angrily.

'Just for repeating something he'd heard, without thinking about it?' said Michael. 'That would be very unfair; we all do it.'

'Why isn't it true?' asked Tony.

'Well, the world isn't an institution,' said Michael.

'And games don't matter except to a few people,' said Ralph. 'And other things matter, that hardly matter here at all.'

'What?' asked George.

'Money and family,' said Ralph, with unction.

'And you needn't go on boring us about games,' said Harry. 'It's not as if you were in the least good at cricket. He'd never get into the Eleven if it was to save his life, would he, Tony?'

'Never,' said Tony.

George burst into tears, and rushed angrily at Harry: 'You, with your foul German aunt!' he said.

'That's his misfortune, hardly his fault,' said Ralph.

Nan Hackett came in, and this stopped the altercation.

'What's all this about?' she said. 'Who's been upsetting George?'

'No one,' said Michael, to whom the question was addressed. 'Harry just happened to mention the fact that he was no good at cricket, and he began to blub.'

'It was very unkind of Harry,' said Miss Hackett. 'George does at least try: he's keen.'

'All the worse, if he tries.'

'I don't understand you, Michael,' said Nan, in a pained voice.

'There's so very little result,' said Michael.

'Well, Harry might do a bit of trying,' said Nan. 'Mr Knight was very much surprised that he didn't go down for a bathe with you others, this evening.'

'I hardly think he can have been surprised,' said Harry.

'Disappointed, I should say,' said Nan. 'No, I think he was surprised too. He's still kind enough to expect the best in you all.'

'He didn't tell me to go,' said Harry. 'It wasn't compulsory.'

'Does everything have to be compulsory?' said Nan. 'Is it compulsory for you to read books you're always reading? Is it compulsory for boys' parents to come down and take them out, or to send them presents?'

'There's no comparison, Miss Hackett,' said Michael. 'People like to do things to please themselves or other people, whether they have to or not. But it's just silly to do something you hate, and that's no good to anyone else, unless you're made to.'

'It's good for all of us to do things we don't like occasionally,' said Nan.

'We all have to do lots of things we don't like every day,' said Michael. 'Harry would never get into the swimming-bath if he didn't have to.'

'Oh, I'm sure that's not true!' protested Nan.

'It's perfectly true,' said Harry.

'Well, it's sometimes wise to do things we don't like now, because of the future,' said Nan. 'I know Mr Knight is worried about you; he is particularly anxious that you should learn to swim before you go to a public school. An extra bathe like this would be just the chance for you to make an effort....'

'I have another summer term here,' said Harry. 'There are two years before there's any question of my having to swim at a public school. There's no hurry.'

'Oh, you never know,' said Nan. 'You never know when you might need to be able to swim: if you went on the river...'

'I should never do such a thing,' said Harry.

'Or if you saw someone drowning,' said Nan.

'That doesn't often happen to people, Miss Hackett,' said Michael. 'And you have to be a very good swimmer to save someone else. Unless you're really good, you should run for help: otherwise there'd be two people to save.'

'And so awful if one did save someone,' said Ralph. 'One would be called "Boy Hero" in the newspapers: one would never live it down.'

'But if you saw someone drown, you'd never forgive yourself,' said Nan.

'I don't see why not, unless you'd pushed them in,' said Harry.

'My dear Miss Hackett, if that ever happens to you, my mother's psychiatrist will put you right in no time,' said Ralph. 'He's expensive, of course.'

83

'Really, you boys are too clever to live,' said Nan. 'And now it's silence time.'

'Nan's right,' said George, when they were in bed. 'Anyone who can't swim is a public danger.'

'Bosh!' said Ralph. 'My grandmother can't swim; few women of her generation ever learned.'

'The people who are a danger are those who can swim a little, and think they're better than they are,' said Michael. 'They're the sort of people who get carried away by currents, and then good swimmers are drowned trying to save them.'

'But some child might drown because Harry couldn't do a few strokes,' said George.

'That's so unlikely, it's not worth considering,' said Harry.

'Anything is worth considering, if a human life is in danger,' said George.

'An imaginary human life, in imaginary danger!' said Michael. 'You shouldn't be so pompous.'

'You're a bit too clever, Park.'

'My dear Girlie, I don't see how one can be.'

'They won't like it at your public school.'

'On the contrary,' said Ralph. 'A public school is a place of education, after all; as you seem to forget. They'll be very proud of Michael, because of course he'll get a scholarship to Oxford or Cambridge. So will Harry. They'll be in the sixth almost at once, and dunces like you will have to clean their boots and make their tea.'

'I shouldn't fancy tea made by George,' said Michael.

'Oh, he'll be out of that stage, before you have a slave,' said Ralph. 'Otherwise he'll be superannuated. I don't mean him, actually, but dunces like him.'

'You'd better not use that word again, Wimbush,' said George. 'What about you?'

'Oh, I shall go to Eton,' said Ralph. 'My father's

family will pay for that. Mother will come down on Sundays with Lords to take me out to luncheon; I shall go down very well there. I think we shall all do very well at our public schools,' he continued generously. 'If George turns out to be a good footballer—and for all we know, he may, as they'll play rugger at his next school —he may have quite a good time. And Tony is a fine cricketer—and any way he's so pretty that the prefects will do anything for a smile from him.'

'Shut up, Ralph!' cried Tony delightedly, throwing a slipper at his head.

'What about Ronald?' asked Harry.

'Among five hundred boys he may not be noticed much,' said Ralph. 'That's his best chance.'

CHAPTER TEN

New every morning is the Love
Our wakening and uprising prove.

This was their morning hymn and perhaps, for it was a bright day, two pairs of eyes looked with refreshed love at Dudley Knight, and other eyes at Tony Stuart; Kit's eyes strayed to the lovely beech tree just outside: *trahit sua quemque voluptas.*

Kit was doing some of MacLeod's work as well as his own. He read the sixth a few pages out of a book about Athens and Sparta, and asked them to write a short essay; comparing and contrasting, establishing a preference for one way of life rather than the other, with reasons for their choice. While they were so engaged, he corrected a pile of French exercises.

'How did you get on with Anita?' said his aunt, after school dinner.

'Oh—Miss Rigby, you mean?' said Kit. 'All right, I hope. Because I think Nan is rather turning against me.'

'At one time I thought you two might be allies,' said Mary.

'Because I'm friends with Matron?' said Kit. 'No, there's rather a split there. Matron and I tried to befriend poor little Harry Staples; Nan started on our side, and now she's gone over to the enemy.'

'Dudley is hard on that boy, I'm afraid,' said Mary.

'And he likes that odious Girling creature, who is his chief tormentor,' added Kit.

'Is that the boy with the nose?' said Mary. 'Yes, of course, I remember now. Well, if Harry has Dudley against him, he'll have Nan too. She'd drown him with her own hands to please Dudley. She's one of the few people I've met, whom I've felt to be capable of murder.'

'Really, Aunt Mary!'

'Yes, you look at her hands, and at her eyes,' said Mary. 'She's remorselessly determined. I shouldn't think Anita had a chance.'

'I suppose it may depend a bit on Dudley,' said Kit.

'A little,' said Mary. 'One doesn't know which type he prefers: their very names describe them. Nan is the mother-nurse type. "Anita" sounds barely respectable; and she is trying to be the courtesan, in rather a home-made sort of way. He's got a mother already—a very evil old hag—and I suppose she may influence events; she would probably dislike one of those girls more than the other. But which?'

'She may keep Dudley single while she lives,' said Kit.

'That's what I rather expect,' said Mary. 'And for all we know, he may meet charming women in the holi-days; one's so prone to think one knows all about a person's life.... But to get back to Anita?'

'She was rather girlish at first,' said Kit. '"Oh, Mr Henderson, isn't this fun?" She even, at an early point, pretended to find the match exciting.'

'I forget who won,' said Mary.

'Oh, there was a draw, as there usually is,' said Kit. 'There wasn't time to play it out. I defy cricket to excite me; but there wasn't any of the sort of thing that excites people who are excited by it.'

'No "breathless hush in the close"?' said Mary.

'No, though they were pretty quiet,' said Kit. 'Hazel-ford is a perfectly beastly school, Aunt Mary. D'you know, they really make them watch the game? A lot of poor little wretches were keeping scores, to prove they had.'

'I suppose Anita went off with her sister,' said Mary.

'Oh, yes, almost at once,' said Kit. 'I was rather touched; I imagined one of the Brontë girls going to visit another in this sort of way.'

'When Wuthering Heights played Thrushcross Grange!' said Mary. 'I don't see Anita as Emily.'

'Oh, she's Anne, and I suppose that's her name,' said Kit. 'The other one made me feel rather said: a little older, a little sadder, and a little more determinedly bright.'

'I wonder if she has someone to love at Hazelford,' said Mary. 'I almost hope so; it passes the time.'

'I didn't see anyone suitable,' said Kit. 'It was rather a young, tough, jolly staff.'

'Odious it sounds,' said Mary. 'Was Anita more confiding on the way home?'

'She rather reproached herself, and nearly reproached me, for having an afternoon's pleasure, when poor Mr Knight was on duty,' he said. 'He was so overburdened —never spared himself—then there was a *sotto voce* reference to "that unfortunate Mr MacLeod". Miss Rigby felt quite worried; there was so little she could do.'

'You don't seem to have mentioned the boys, either of you.'

'No, I don't think we spoke about them at all,' said Kit.

'I find that very healthy,' said Mary. 'I like Anita much better than Nan. I think she does as little harm as any human creature here.'

Nan, meanwhile, was confiding to Dudley her misgivings about the boys in the Grey Room.

'It's not exactly anything one can take hold of,' she

said. 'In a way one should be proud that they're such clever boys. But sometimes one feels something isn't quite right. As Matron says: "They're so sharp they could cut themselves." '

'Ah, Nan, and I fear they will,' said Dudley.

'I suppose there's no need to worry,' said Nan. 'They're going through a phase.'

'It depends,' said Dudley. 'Nan—er—do you think they know more than they ought to know? Forgive me for raising a delicate point—but do you think their purity is quite unbesmirched?'

'Oh, I wouldn't dream of suggesting that it was anything like that,' said Nan. 'I see no reason at all to think that.'

Dudley heaved a sigh, almost of disappointment. 'I don't quite understand what worries you,' he continued.

'I hardly understand myself,' she said. 'It's a sort of spirit of criticism. I daresay it is a good thing; but it hardly seems right in quite such young boys. One feels they should take more from one on trust....'

'Hm,' said Dudley. 'I think some influence is at work. What would you say if I were to suggest that they were trying, in their childish way, to imitate young Henderson?'

'I'm sure he wouldn't do them any harm,' said Nan.

'Not wilfully, not directly,' said Dudley. 'Christopher is a fine young chap, and anxious to do his duty by his good uncle. But the question is: is he quite the best person to have charge of boys at that stage in their development?'

'There's nothing to do about it,' said Nan. 'We have to have him here till the end of the term; and he won't stay any longer.'

'Oh, Nan, I never meant that we should wish him to go,' said Dudley. 'I only said that the question was if he was the best person to have here. And there is something that can be done. One can keep a special eye on boys who seem to be coming under his influence. And one can say a word in season to friend Christopher, if it seems indicated. I have found him quite reasonable.'

'What about asking the headmaster to say a word to him?' said Nan.

'No, Nan; I'd rather have it out with him directly,' said Dudley. 'I like to be quite frank and open in these things. Besides, I'm not quite sure that the headmaster would welcome any criticism of his nephew. He's proud of him, and rightly. We all expect great things of him at Cambridge.'

'I've wanted to talk to you about some of the junior boys in the sixth form,' began Dudley.

'Yes, sir; yes, I mean,' said Kit. 'They're clever boys, some of them. You should have a fine sixth form next year, and you ought to get two scholarships.'

'Park and Staples, yes,' said Dudley. 'But that's not all; what do you think of their development in other things?'

'I'm not quite sure what you mean,' said Kit. 'I'm hardly qualified to say much about them: I just do French with them, and some of poor MacLeod's work. By the way, Ralph Wimbush's French is quite excellent.'

'Ah, don't let's beg the question, Christopher,' said Dudley. 'How d'you think these boys are getting on, in the difficult process of passing from childhood to adolescence?'

'I suppose they are taking things as they come,' said Kit. 'I don't talk to them about that sort of thing.'

'They don't bring their problems to you?' said Dudley. 'I thought they might, as you are nearer to them in age.'

'Not problems of that sort,' said Kit. 'If they did, I should send them to my uncle.'

'Quite right,' said Dudley. 'But I have sometimes thought one or two of them might have difficulties. Now that boy, Staples; he doesn't always seem quite a happy boy.'

'Poor Harry!' said Kit. 'I'm afraid there's been a general conspiracy to make him terrified of his public school.'

'He's not the type of boy to be happy there,' said Dudley. 'But friend Staples has got a year in which to pull up his socks.'

'I've tried to make him feel rather better about it,' said Kit. 'I told him he'd pass in high, and go into the sixth in two years or less. Then he'll be all right, you know. In any civilized school he'll be respected then. It's up to his house-master to look after him a bit at first, and to adapt things a little so that life is not intolerable for him.'

'I'd rather think about Staples adjusting himself to a public school, rather than about a great school adapting itself to him,' said Dudley, grimly.

'Oh, I'm sure there will have to be a bit of give-and-take,' said Kit. 'But after all the school exists for the boys, not the boys for the school. Any way, the thing I wanted to do was to cheer him up a bit.'

'I appreciate your kind intention,' said Dudley. 'I hope I give it full weight. But what I wonder is: is it the kindest thing to make the future sound too rosy for Harry Staples?'

'I hardly think I did that,' said Kit. 'I never pretended that he wouldn't find difficulties ahead of him. But my own experience of school has shown me that a boy with his brains is sure to find a place of his own, somehow.'

'A place of his own,' repeated Dudley; 'but isn't that

the danger? Isn't it possible that he will contrive to live on some sort of island of his own, and out of the main stream of school-life?'

'I think that is his best hope,' said Kit.

'Come, Christopher,' said Dudley, taking his arm. 'You don't really think that? When a boy goes to one of our great schools, and is subject to the finest educational system now existing—perhaps the finest the world has ever known—you can't really think that he should withdraw from all the fellowship and all the life about him to live selfishly on a little island, with all that flood of vigorous life surging round him, but passing him by?'

'He won't be able to isolate himself to any harmful extent,' said Kit. 'But I do think Harry will be happier if he sits a bit aloof from school life—and I think in a good school he will find that he can.'

'Events will show,' murmured Dudley. 'I'm conceited enough to call this a good school, and I feel doubts about his happiness here.'

'I think he has been unhappy because of his fear of his next school,' said Kit. 'I think I have taken away a good deal of that. Then, he was frightened in the swimming-bath; but my uncle has seen that it's no use taking him in the belt. He just goes into the bath as a form, and knows he won't be bothered—and that has made him happier.'

'Happier because he's been given up as a bad job!' said Dudley.

'Isn't it better to recognize failure?' said Kit. 'I think it is almost a test of intelligence, to know an impossibility when one sees it.'

'Oh, my dear Christopher!' said Dudley. 'What a dreadful thing to say! It's dogged that does it. That's what I've been taught; and there's no such word as "can't".'

'I think the boy could learn, but in different conditions,' said Kit. 'I think they're for his parents to arrange, if they wish it.'

'I know what I should like to prescribe for friend Staples,' said Dudley. 'His father's abroad; but I might have a talk with his good aunt. I should like him to go somewhere for a month with a holiday tutor—someone who's just finished school, like yourself, but more on the athletic side. I'd send them to a seaside place where they could start every day with a bathe before breakfast. Then—afterwards, they could do a round or two of boxing, and a little net practice.'

Kit was silent.

'Staples would be another boy, after a week or two,' said Dudley. 'They couldn't do much in the way of football,' he added regretfully. 'But I suppose he could improve his dribbling....'

'It wouldn't be much of a holiday for him,' said Kit.

'Many boys would love it,' said Dudley.

'Some might; but Harry would not,' said Kit. 'And what's the use of his boxing? Only women think boys get on the gloves when they quarrel. In fact, they're like ancient Greek pancratists: they scratch and kick and bite. It's true that he might quite enjoy giving George Girling one on the nose.'

Dudley laughed, without amusement. 'Poor old George!' he said. 'I fancy there's no love lost between those two. But you know, if Harry uses his wits to tease old George, it's not so unfair if George uses his muscles.'

'He's certainly not got any wits,' said Kit. 'But I don't think it's like that. George and that horrible Ronald Gibson have got hold of some story they plague Harry about.'

'I must go into this,' said Dudley gravely. 'I had a hint of it once before from Nan Hackett.'

'I wish you wouldn't,' said Kit, regretting his imprudence. 'I don't think Harry would like it. I've talked about it to Matron, and we agreed that it ought to be allowed to die a natural death. The other boys in the room, Michael Park, Ralph Wimbush and Tony Stuart are on Harry's side; so is Hugh Tupholme.'

'Ah, Tony Stuart; that's a nice lad!' said Dudley tenderly.

'By the way,' said Kit. 'There's something I meant to speak to you about before. I hope you won't mind. But you know my uncle put me in charge of the swimming-bath? This morning, Matron and I found the padlock open in the gate, and she didn't quite like it. She said you had let some of the boys have an extra bathe on Saturday evening.'

'Quite right to mention it, Christopher,' said Dudley. 'Of course I have a key, and so has your uncle—but I ought to have seen that it was locked up. I'm afraid I just let the boys be on their own.'

'On their own, in the swimming-bath?' said Kit with surprise.

'Oh, they were responsible fellows,' said Dudley. 'I left Michael Park in charge. Good for them to run things for themselves now and then.'

'They didn't lock the gate,' Kit reminded him.

Dudley had to wait a day or two before he could find a favourable moment to talk to George Girling alone. The boys had so very little free time that it was not often possible to see one of them alone for fifteen minutes on end. If the headmaster had a boy to his study, it was for a beating, and that was quickly over.

'Push George Girling along to my room, Wimbush, will you?' he said to Ralph.

'You're for it, Girlie,' said Ralph. 'Deadly Nightshade wants you in his lair.'

'I daresay he just wants to give George some advice about his nose,' said someone. 'It's a disgrace to the school to have a nose that you could grow cabbages in.'

'George, I know how fond you all are of Mr Henderson,' said Dudley. 'It's a great thing for you to have a young man fresh from school, and so gifted as he is, too.'

'Yes, sir,' said George.

'Do I hear a faint note of disagreement?' said Dudley with a smile. 'Of course, I could never permit any boy to criticize another master to me—you quite understand? —And I should never dream of criticizing another member of the staff in talking to any of the boys.'

'Of course not, sir.'

'And here, at Hazelcroft, we trust our masters and mistresses; we leave them to do their own work in their own way. We don't ask questions or pry.'

'Of course not, sir.'

'Now, what I wanted to ask you about was Harry Staples,' said Dudley. 'You see, I trust your judgement more than that of some of the so called "clever boys". I do hope and believe that Mr Henderson has managed to help that poor boy, and make him happier. I felt I'd like to talk to you about it for a minute, so as to know how to go on with the good work after Mr Henderson has left us.'

'He's talked to Harry,' said George. 'He's talked to him in rather a grownup way.'

'That may have been very wise,' said Dudley. 'And Harry is definitely happier, I think; he's less worried than he used to be about his next school.'

'Yes,' said George.

'You don't seem altogether in favour?' said Dudley, smiling.

'Harry's getting a swelled head,' said George. 'Mr Henderson told him he might be happier at a public school, because there were sure to be several first class brains on the staff—and Harry seems to think no one else fit to talk to him.'

Dudley appeared strangely moved. He got up and paced about the room.

'Hm,' he said, almost to himself. 'The man is young; hardly more than a boy. We must remember that.' He struck his hand on the desk. 'What does he know about older men, and their disappointments? Better men than he have failed to fulfil their first promise.'

George was sitting in embarrassment on the edge of his chair.

'Forgive me,' said Dudley, with a smile. 'I was thinking aloud for a moment. And you will not think I have criticized Mr Henderson if I have said that he is young —because that is a thing you must have seen for yourself!'

'Yes, sir.'

'Then, there's another thing, George, in connection with Harry Staples,' said Dudley. 'Miss Hackett has told me that there is something that you and Ronald Gibson keep ragging him about. I want to know: what is it?'

'I don't want to say, sir,' said George.

'Girling, you are a scout,' said Dudley. 'You have taken a solemn oath to obey the orders of your scoutmaster without question. I am your scoutmaster, and I order you, on your scout's honour, to tell me what this is about. It shall remain a secret between us.'

There was no help for it; and perhaps George did not very much desire help.

'I suppose I shouldn't have ragged Harry,' he owned. 'But he's younger than me, and he's been cheeky to me.' ('Cheek' by Hazelcroft standards was strictly a matter of age: you might say pretty well what you liked to a boy only a week younger than yourself, but if he were so much as a month older he would resent it as 'cheek'). George now poured out his grievances about superannuation, and Harry's criticism of his cricket.

'That doesn't come well from him,' said Dudley. 'If

there ever was a rabbit! And I doubt if he even tries.'

Then, gradually, the story of the 'German aunt' came out.

'You shouldn't have ragged him about that,' said Dudley. 'A boy isn't responsible for his connections; and, any way, the lady is my very good friend. She may have some foreign blood; but her husband did great service to this country during the war, remember, and received a knighthood for it.'

George hung his head, then, reviving a little, he told Dudley the story that Ralph and Harry had elaborated in the sick-room. He simplified it a little, so that it was now told in the form of fact rather than conjecture, and Ralph's part-authorship was not mentioned.

'What a mischievous little liar that boy seems to be!' said Dudley. 'To make up a tissue of falsehood like that, about a kind lady who has had him to stay in her beautiful home!'

'You won't say anything about it, sir?' said George uneasily. 'You promised me that it should remain a secret.'

'I'm afraid, I made a rash promise, George,' said Dudley. 'That was very wrong. I'm afraid I've fallen beneath the standard I set myself. I give you the right to remind me of it whenever you like. You see, this isn't a thing I have a right to keep secret, is it? I ought to break my promise; oughtn't I? What was wrong was to make it. I can't allow the name of this lady, my very good friend, to be maligned, can I?'

The eyes of Dudley seemed to ask a question of his soul, and George lied in the soul, and said 'Yes.'

'I knew you would release me from my promise,' said Dudley, which was putting it rather differently.

In spite of his scout's promise, George felt disinclined to reveal the theory that Dudley designed to marry Lady Best-Pennant; and he was now convinced of its truth.

CHAPTER ELEVEN

On a thundery morning, the headmaster seemed to have caught the mood of the day. Some boys were in tears, and the rest of them in a state of acute apprehension. One boy had had a ruler broken over his head, and another had been swung right and left by the dewlaps.

'If ever there was a heartless class!' groaned Mr Langton.

They were doing problems in Arithmetic: pasture and growing grass.

'Gracious heaven, Tony!' exclaimed Mr Langton. 'Do you realize what you have put down as the daily consumption of grass per cow? One cubic acre!'

He seized the boy by the nape of the neck, and thrust down his head in the direction of his deplorable exercise book; Tony neatly avoided hitting his forehead on the lid of the desk, and emerged on all fours between the legs.

Mr Langton was restored to good humour, and roared with laughter. At this moment a clap of thunder and a sudden downpour cleared the air.

It was thought worth while to let the boys change after school dinner, in case cricket should be possible.

'Gosh, it's got hot again!' said Tony.

'Let's have another meeting of the Purity League,' said Michael, flinging off all his clothes.

Before anyone else could follow his example, Nan Hackett was in the room.

'What is the meaning of this exhibition?' she asked. 'Take five conduct marks, Michael.'

'Oh, Miss Hackett!' said Michael, covering his nakedness with a towel. 'I've got three garments on! That's the rule of the Purity League—never less than three garments.'

'Don't be silly, Michael,' said Nan. 'You've been behaving in a very rude and childish way; it's not at all what one expects of the head-boy in a senior room.'

'I'm sorry, Miss Hackett.'

'The headmaster and Mr Knight will be very much surprised.'

Dudley Knight was not, indeed, much surprised, but he expressed pain.

'Very trying for you, dear Nan,' he said. 'Now, if I had my way, those bigger boys wouldn't be in a woman's province at all.'

'Mr Knight, I've trained in hospital as a probationer,' said Nan. 'I help Matron with the boys' baths. I don't need taking care of.'

'Hm,' said Dudley. 'I hope there was no reason to suppose that there was going to be any—er—beastliness?'

'Oh, no, Mr Knight!' said Nan.

'Did you put that to Park?'

'Oh, no,' said Nan. 'I'm afraid I never thought of that. Ought I to have?'

'If there was, he'd only have denied it,' said Dudley. 'And it isn't for a woman to cope with such things.'

'I am sure it was only a silly game,' said Nan.

'Then the others were going to play?' said Dudley eagerly.

'We don't know at all,' said Nan. 'Don't you think it would be a mistake to treat it as something serious?'

'I don't know, Nan, I don't know,' said Dudley mournfully. 'Perhaps it's of no importance at all; but

99

perhaps it's symptomatic. At the same time I find other odd things going on in that room. I discover that friend Staples has been amusing his friends with a lot of libellous fairy-tales about his good aunt, Lady Best-Pennant, who is a personal friend of mine.'

'Oh, I expect it has got exaggerated in the repetition,' said Nan. 'Boys are real old women for gossip. So that's what George and Ronald were always teasing him about? He would never say.'

'He'd be ashamed to say,' said Dudley. 'And well he might!'

'Well, it's a relief to know it was only that,' said Nan.

'Only that!' said Dudley. 'I'm afraid I can't think it a trivial thing that one of our boys should try to make himself interesting by spinning a criminally libellous yarn about someone to whom he only owes gratitude—and a friend of my own too.'

'I don't know why you want to connect these two episodes, Mr Knight,' said Nan. 'They seem to me so different.'

'Nan, they are both instances of very irresponsible conduct by boys from the same group—younger boys in the sixth form. They are episodes of a sort that I'm glad to say I can't remember in my time here before. They take place at the same time. I can't help asking myself if there is any connection between them. I pray they may be unconnected, for I can only guess at one possible connecting link.'

'What?'

'Nan,' said Dudley gently. 'What has distinguished this term from all other terms?'

'Poor Mr MacLeod's collapse.'

'No, I didn't mean that, Nan; and I don't think you thought I did,' said Dudley, in a tender cooing voice. 'You know I meant that this term we've had Christopher Henderson here.'

'Oh, Mr Knight, that isn't fair!' exclaimed Nan.

'I'm not saying that he has any connection with these episodes,' said Dudley. 'I know he can have none of a direct kind. But I notice he comes here, and then odd things happen among boys whom I believe to be attached to him. Can I help asking myself if he is a subversive influence in the school?'

'Oh, I can't think that!'

'Nan,' said Dudley. 'You mustn't think I blame the boy—young Christopher, I mean—in any way. I like him personally. I just wonder if he's the right man in the right place. You know, sometimes I'm afraid our excellent headmaster is getting a little past things. It's a question whether the school won't begin to go down, if he can't see his way to pull out in time. Of course you will treat this as just said between ourselves?'

'Of course.'

Later in the day, Dudley found Harry on the edge of the cricket field.

'Well, Staples, I'd like a word with you,' he said. 'You're not supposed to be doing anything, are you?'

'No, sir, we're in,' said Harry.

'Well, we'll take a little turn,' said Dudley. 'They'll shout if they want you, I suppose? I wanted to talk to you about rather a delicate subject—this silly nonsense about your so-called German aunt.'

Dudley's voice hardened. 'I understand you have been trying to make yourself interesting by romancing to other boys about a lady who has been most kind to you. She has several times had you to stay in her beautiful home, though your connection with her is not of the nearest. I have been grieved and shocked to hear that you have tried to turn her into a villainess of cheap fiction; that you have even suggested that she is guilty of murder. Do you know the seriousness of your action? Or how severely it is punished by the law?'

'Oh, sir; I never said that,' said Harry.

'My information is that you did,' said Dudley. 'Are you prepared to swear that you did not?'

'Certainly,' said Harry, determined, but trembling. 'I cannot be responsible for your information. It comes from Ronald Gibson, and he is a liar.'

'Those are strong words, Staples,' said Dudley. 'And let me tell you that your story did not come to me from Ronald Gibson.'

'Who was it, then?'

'That I mustn't say,' said Dudley. 'And does it matter?'

'No, sir,' said Harry bravely. 'I know better what I said than any other person could. And whoever told you this story must have got it second-hand from Ronald Gibson. Ronald was pretending to be asleep, and was listening to Ralph and me talking in the sickroom—we did talk about my aunt and cousins, and why shouldn't we?'

'That is your account of things, is it?' said Dudley. 'I get the impression that there has been much more talk about the subject than that.'

'Only Ronald Gibson and George Girling have spoken to me about it since then,' said Harry. 'They wanted to annoy me.'

'So you persist in your story?' said Dudley. 'Let me tell you what I think. I think this term you've begun to find some of your lessons more amusing. You have come to turn some of your old ideas topsy turvey, and to give free vein to your imagination—oh, I don't say it's altogether a bad thing. But then the danger arises. Mayn't a moment come when we can no longer tell good from bad, or truth from falsehood?'

'I think you are talking about Mr Henderson's

lessons, sir,' said Harry. 'He has never known any of this story; I didn't want to tell him. It has nothing to do with him. I hadn't even met him that day when Ralph and I were talking in the sickroom.'

'I wish I could believe you,' said Dudley. 'But I get such very different accounts. I don't mean, of course, that anyone has mentioned Mr Henderson, and you do wrong to bring up his name. But I think this relapse of yours into childishness has something to do with your work this term; I don't think it just happened on that first day of term in the sickroom. Just think very carefully, Staples; let your mind travel over the past month. I think you'll find you agree with me—and, if you'll admit it, we need say no more.'

Harry perceived that he was being offered a dishonest bargain, and one by which he had little to gain.

'I cannot admit what is not true,' he said. 'And there is nothing more that can be said: you could not tell my aunt.'

'You need not be too sure of that, Harry,' said Dudley.

'I don't think you will, sir,' said Harry in exhaustion. 'I don't know what you could find to say.'

At evening prayers Dudley cooed in his tenderest tone: 'Grant that the friendships formed between us here may neither through sin be broken, nor hereafter through worldly cares be forgotten, but that drawn together by the unseen chain of Thy love we be brought *nearer* to Thee, and *nearer* to each other ...'

Mrs Langton was even with him, and they sang:

> *Blest are the pure in heart,*
> *For they shall see our God ...*

There was plenty to talk about at Supper (the staff dined at mid day, with the boys). Matron supped upstairs, so her kindly influence was lacking.

'It's been a disappointing day,' said Dudley, with a sigh. 'A day on which one is almost tempted to lose heart.'

'Oh, that's not like you, Mr Knight!' said Miss Rigby.

Nan sighed, and turned her eyes sadly towards Dudley, who was on her left. It was seen that she wished it to be seen that she shared his sorrow.

'It's been a heavy, thundery day,' said Mrs Langton.

'Very close,' said Dudley. 'But that's not it.'

'Have the boys been up to something?' said Mrs Langton. 'Boys will, of course, be boys, and very trying it is. But how should we all make our living if they weren't?'

Dudley was sad and hesitant, and wondered if he could speak before 'the ladies'.

'"The ladies" always know the worst,' said Mary Langton. 'Any way, Nan saw it with her own eyes, and it was nothing so very dreadful: only dear little Michael in the state of Nature. Rather sweet.'

'I think he should be deposed from being head of the room, Headmaster,' said Dudley. 'He doesn't show a sense of responsibility. Now George Girling is a few months older, and steadier altogether.'

'I won't have that dunce put over clever boys,' said Langton.

'He's a bully, as well as a dunce,' said Kit. 'I've found him plaguing the life out of Harry Staples.'

'You know my maxim,' said Dudley. 'If there's a case of bullying, punish the boy who is being bullied twice as much as the bully. If boys take it into their own hands to deal with each other, they generally have a reason.'

'I can't agree with you there, Knight,' said Dick Langton.

'What do you think is behind this story?' said Dudley. 'It would be laughable if it wasn't tragic. That wretched boy Staples has invented a long rigmarole about his aunt, Lady Best-Pennant. He's been amusing other boys with a penny dreadful romance. He says she mastered Sir William, turned his daughters out of the house, and forced him to make a will leaving her everything. He maintains that he has never gone quite so far as to accuse her of murdering his uncle, though my information says that he did.'

'And how do you know that the story may not be substantially true, Mr Knight?' said Mary Langton. 'Does your information go as far as that?'

'A lot of odd things go on in families,' said the headmaster.

'Really, I must protest!' said Dudley. 'A lady I know personally...'

'So do we,' said Mrs Langton.

'In any case, it's no business of that Girling boy's,' said Kit.

'Boys who invent romances of this kind deserve to be unmercifully ragged,' said Dudley.

'He has been,' said Kit. 'Anyhow, the boy will never be bullied about this again; I shall see to that.'

'Oh, you will, will you?' said Dudley.

'Don't you want me to?' said Kit.

'Oh, yes, of course, Christopher,' said Dudley. 'I think you may be the right person, as you are rather in his confidence. I just wanted to know what line you meant to take....'

'I shall tell him that all is known.'

'He knows that,' said Dudley. 'I had my word with him.'

'Then he must know that his blackmailers have given away his secret to Authority,' said Kit. 'They have no threat or weapon left.'

'I don't like the word "blackmail" applied to a fine chap like Girling,' said Dudley. 'And it's inaccurate. No one tried to get money or anything else out of Staples.'

'I should dislike George Girling and Ronald Gibson less if they had been after money,' said Kit. 'Money can do some positive good; they simply wanted to be cruel, which is only negative and evil.'

'You always have your own way of looking at things, Christopher,' said Dudley, in a cold voice. 'I hope the boys are not adversely affected by it.'

'If Harry has been silly, he's learned his lesson,' said Mary.

'I gave him quite a bad quarter of an hour,' said Dudley.

'And what's going to happen to George?' said Mary.

'I shall speak to him,' said her husband. 'If there's any more nonsense about this, he shall get six of the best— and from the gardener, who's a stronger man than I am.'

'Poor old George!' said Miss Rigby, smiling across the table at Dudley. 'Really he's beginning to paint very nicely.'

'The gardener will make him black and blue, if there's any more trouble from him,' said Dick Langton.

'I'd admire Staples more if he took it into his own hands,' said Dudley.

'"Revenge is a certain wild justice",' quoted Mary. 'But I prefer the garden variety.'

'Administered by the gardener,' said Kit.

'What nonsense it is to say bullies are always cowards,' said Mary. 'In all my considerable experience not one has been.'

'Though it is true that the Girling creature is reduced to tears by the least little pain,' put in Kit.

'Boys who are bullied are cowards,' said Dudley. 'Otherwise they wouldn't stand for it.'

'They stand for it much more than they should,' said Mary. 'It ought to be reported to Authority at once.'

'The boys would call that "sneaking",' said Nan.

'I thoroughly approve of sneaking,' said Mary. 'Among grownup people it is almost the first duty of a good citizen. This ridiculous school ethic ought to be done away with, it unfits boys for life.'

'You don't think it right and natural, at the boys' present stage of development?' asked Dudley.

'I don't think it's right at all,' said Mary. 'And we all know it's not in the least bit natural; very young children are always "telling on" each other. They learn not to here; it's one of the ways in which we corrupt their innocence.'

'Whether George Girling is a coward or not, I shall put the fear of God into him all right,' said the headmaster.

'I think boys who are continually bullied become very brave,' said Kit. 'I mean, they acquire more than ordinary powers of endurance, because they need them in their daily life. I believe Harry could endure all things—he's the stuff of which martyrs are made.'

'You don't mean all this clever nonsense,' said Dudley in a pleading tone. 'You don't really mean it, Christopher. I know, among ourselves, it's very amusing. You like to throw down a paradox and watch it explode. But not before the boys, please. *Maxima debetur puero reverentia*, you know.'

'I know a little Latin too,' said Kit. '*Quis custodiet ipsos custodes?* Who's to keep an eye on those who have to keep an eye on others?'

CHAPTER TWELVE

'Your essays were very interesting,' said Kit to the sixth form. 'There's only time to talk about one or two of them. Harry Staples gets full marks; I think his is the most original.'

Harry had painted Sparta very black indeed, but he thought that Athens also spent too much time and trouble on gymnastics. He decided that, on the whole, he would have chosen to be born a Spartan, for then he would certainly have been exposed at birth—while in Athens they would very likely have given him a chance as a first-born son. He imagined that a very young infant had only a slender hold upon life, and that it would all have been over quickly and almost painlessly.

Kit laughed. 'It's a dangerous sort of essay to write,' he said. 'Some examiners would be furious with you and give you nought.'

Michael had written a sensible and well-planned eulogy of Athens.

'But I don't care for some of your language,' said Kit. 'You say: "Periclean Athens was confessedly the high-water-mark of civilization"—you wouldn't talk like that. And why "confessedly"? What does it mean? Who confesses it? And why "confess"? It's not a damaging admission.'

'It's what Mr Knight once told us.'

'I expect he was quoting from a book,' said Kit. 'I don't think that sort of language mixes well with our own style, which is plain and forthright and very good. I think, if you quote what other people say, you would do well to put it into your own language first.'

Ralph had drawn a picture of a beautiful, sybaritic Athens, where young men of family had nothing to do but to amuse themselves: this they did in accordance with their tastes, some watched wrestling, others ate grapes and listened to flute-playing, others talked.

'I think Athenian life must often have been more strenuous than that,' said Kit.

'Oh,' said Ralph naughtily. 'I thought they just led a life of ease, while slaves toiled for their comfort.'

Everyone laughed, except George Girling, who scowled with disapproval. He had written a dull essay, praising the Spartans for their love of physical fitness, because they knew how to defend themselves, and because they—in fact—won the war against Athens.

Kit spoke of this essay, not for its merits, but because it was the only one of its kind.

'Don't you think they overdid it, a bit;' said Kit. 'After all, no one was particularly likely to attack them in their valley.'

'I bet it was hideous, sir,' said Ralph.

'No,' said Kit. 'You'd expect that, wouldn't you? But the headmaster and Mrs Langton have been there; they tell me it's extremely beautiful, and wildly romantic.'

'That would make life possible there,' said Guy.

'I'll come to your essay in a moment,' said Kit. He went on to suggest to George that the cult of physical fitness could be exaggerated as much as anything else, and that in Sparta it seemed to have excluded other interests and made them a dull people. For one eminent Spartan, anyone could easily name ten or twenty eminent Athenians. Then he spoke of the tedium of camp life, of the horror of the secret police, and of the cruel initiatory rites for young men.

Guy had written an essay that was a passionate hymn to friendship; this, he thought, had been the principle of life both in Athens and in Sparta. He maintained that a pair of lovers could be equally happy under either dispensation, though for one man alone Sparta had nothing to offer.

Kit wished to be gentle with him, and not to expose him to the laughter of the others. 'I think there is a great deal in what you say,' he said delicately. 'But you are really showing the great superiority of Athens, aren't you, by everything you've said?'

He went on to say that in a happy society one was not so dependent on other people, for life had so much of interest and value to give; it was the unhappy who had to comfort each other, and who might become too dependent upon that comfort.

'"Drawn nearer to each other",' quoted Ralph.

'That's enough from you!' said Kit, but with a twinkle in his eye.

George Girling found himself walking down to the cricket field with Dudley Knight, a happening of no infrequent occurrence.

'Sir, didn't you once tell us that the public school system was based on Sparta?' asked George.

'I hardly think I could have said quite that,' said Dudley. 'It grew up in this country from reforms made in our existing system by Dr Arnold of Rugby. Of course Greek and Roman ideals have come in to it too.... But why do you ask me this?'

'We did an essay the other day on Athens and Sparta for Mr Henderson,' said George. 'He read us a bit from a book, and then asked us to compare them. He didn't seem to think much of Sparta.'

'Hm,' said Dudley. 'I shall be most interested to see those essays.'

Nothing was easier. Like Kit, Dudley now did some

of MacLeod's work, and therefore the English exercises of the sixth form were open to him.

One day he dictated Kipling's *If* to them, and asked them to write a reproduction of it, expressing their own views on it. He then collected their exercise-books for correction.

Kit and his uncle had been sauntering in the garden, now in its midsummer splendour.

'I shall miss this place when I go,' said the head-master. 'I wonder if Knight will bother to keep up the garden?'

'He's got no feeling for it,' said Kit. 'You must stay on as long as you can, Uncle Dick. I've not been here two months yet, but I've come to care for the place. And I've got to like some of the boys; I wouldn't like to leave them to Dudley's mercy.'

'You don't seem to worry about my mercy,' said the headmaster. 'But it's not everyone who would call me a merciful man.'

'I'm not afraid of those who can kill the body—and I know you wouldn't—but of those who can kill the soul,' said Kit. 'I'm very much afraid of them; there are no sanctions to deter them.'

'The boys sing nicely,' said Langton, who had not been listening to him. 'Rotten song, though.'

The singing-lesson was in progress, and had released the staff from duty.

> *Come, here's to Robin Hood*
> *Of the merry gree-een wood,*
> *And a blessing on his name!*

'Knight's not such a bad chap,' said Dick Langton. 'Mixed up about sex, of course, poor fellow—broods over it and hints about it to the boys. They're children still; it can't mean anything to them except theoretically. Of course they think love and all that is slop; and between you and me, that's pretty much what a man comes to think when it's all over.'

'You're just the right age to teach boys, Uncle Dick.'

'Of course,' said Dick Langton. 'Nonsense to say a man is too old, so long as he has his health and his wits.'

They were met by Dudley, with a dozen exercise-books under his arm; he asked if he might speak to them in private.

'Come to my study, Knight,' said Dick Langton. 'Now what's all this about?'

'It's about as serious as it can be,' said Dudley mournfully. 'There's the boy, Guy Tracy, and there's the boy Tony Stuart: and it's got to stop.'

'You can hardly ask me to put an end to their existence,' said Dick Langton.

'Headmaster, almost it might be better if I could!' said Dudley.

'I'm sure it hasn't even begun!' said Kit.

'So, you know something about this affair?' said Dudley accusingly.

'There's nothing to know,' said Kit. 'We've all known that Guy had a sort of childish crush on Tony. I think my aunt first told me.'

'I seem to have been deliberately kept in the dark,' said Dudley.

'Anyone could have noticed,' said Dick Langton. 'One doesn't want to embarrass children by talking about these things, unless their behaviour becomes really silly. They're very natural, and die a natural death.'

'Guy is leaving at the end of this term, any way,' said Kit.

'Natural!' said Dudley.

'Oh, yes, Knight,' said Langton. 'Have the lads done anything silly? Why have you suddenly taken this up?'

'I read this mawkish essay by Tracy,' said Dudley.

'Written for Christopher, here. I saw something was wrong, and I tapped my sources of information, and learned about Tony Stuart.'

'Christopher can't help what boys write for him,' said Langton. 'What was Guy's essay about?'

'Friendship at Athens and Sparta,' said Dudley. 'All about friends (he calls them "lovers") going through life hand in hand. I consider that Christopher was remiss in not drawing our attention to it.'

'I can't see that,' said Dick Langton. 'I'm not a classical man myself; I thought you taught them to admire that sort of thing.'

'I did tell Guy I thought his essay a little exaggerated,' said Kit. 'I suggested to him that there were many other interests in life in Athens; I don't know what else there was in Sparta.'

Dudley made a sound of disgust.

'And what sort of work have they done for you?' said the headmaster, as if dismissing the subject.

'I dictated Kipling's *If* to them,' said Dudley. 'I wanted them to have a fine contemporary poem before them. And I asked them to write about it.'

'I should hardly call it a poem,' said Kit.

'I can't bear all those conditional clauses,' said Dick Langton. 'And then, such a tame conclusion.'

Dudley hissed that some people thought it the high-water-mark of contemporary poetry, and that this was the sort of thing to put before boys as an ideal.

'What did they make of it?' asked Kit.

Most of them had thought it very fine, Dudley told them. Boys generally responded to good stuff once you got them down to it. But there seemed to be a critical attitude that he didn't altogether like to see.

'Why not; when you asked them for criticism?' said Kit.

Dudley had asked for 'appreciation', which he believed to mean praise. One or two of the boys had remarked that they had always been brought up to believe that betting was wrong and foolish, and that anyone who risked his all on one turn of pitch and toss deserved what was coming to him, and would be well advised not to breathe a word about his folly.

'Very sound!' cried Dick Langton delightedly. 'Betting's a mug's game!'

'Don't you think it a little worldly wise?' asked Dudley.

Then one or two of them (and Guy was among them) had protested that a man must be a heartless brute if 'loving friends' were unable to hurt him. Such a one was unfit to have friends, and could not, indeed, know what friendship was.

'That's very good!' said Kit. 'I think they've really put their finger on what makes *If* so horrible; I've never bothered to analyse it for myself. I always felt that, though some of the stoical philosophy in it is all right, in a crudish way, the personality behind it was thoroughly unpleasant....'

Dudley swelled. 'They haven't learned all this from you, Christopher?'

'No, I feel I've learnt something from them,' said Kit.

'I'm uneasy,' said Dudley. 'Frankly I'm uneasy. Boys don't seem any more to be the simple, natural fellows I'm used to. Far be it from me to suggest that any unhealthy influence has lately come into this school....'

'Then don't suggest it, Knight,' said the headmaster shortly. 'As for Guy Tracy, my wife will have a quiet word with him. I take it you've said nothing?'

'I would not, without your approval, Headmaster.'

'I hope not,' said Langton. 'My wife will just say that he doesn't want to make himself conspicuous, or Tony either. No boy wants that.'

'Won't that drive it underground?' said Dudley.

'My dear Knight, you speak as if our boys weren't under constant supervision,' said Langton. 'We know exactly where any boy is at any minute by day or night. No Jesuit college on the Continent can be better supervised.'

'And you appear to have your secret police,' said Kit.

'Not that!' said Dudley. 'But I do like to keep in touch with what the boys are saying and thinking, and some fellows like to tell me these things.'

'Well, I hope I've set your mind at rest,' said Langton, in a tone of dismissal. 'Let's go and have our coffee.'

'Uncle Dick,' said Kit, when he was alone with him. 'If I were a parent—I know the idea's absurd....'

'No, my boy,' said his uncle. 'You're the only member of the staff who has the remotest chance of being one; and you'd make a good one.'

'I wouldn't like a boy of mine to be in Knight's care.'

'Oh, I think we can prevent him from doing any real harm to boys of their age here,' said Dick Langton. 'At any rate while I'm here.'

'But after you the deluge!' said Kit.

It was another Saturday afternoon. Mr Langton himself had gone with the Eleven to Hazelford, where the headmaster was a friend of his.

Michael, Ralph and Harry were idling round the fringe of the cricket field.

'Tony was rather upset,' said Michael. 'Mrs Langton told him that she didn't want to see him and Guy quite so much in each other's pockets.'

'Enough to put him off his game today,' said Harry.

'They're not always together,' said Ralph. 'It's nothing like Philip and Horatio last year. They used to kiss each other, till Matron said she didn't think the headmaster would like it.'

'Rather soft, all this lovey dovey!' said Michael. 'Like a girls' school. My sister seems to spend most of her spare time billing and cooing.'

'But there, I expect the mistresses join in, too,' said Ralph.

'Do they not!' said Michael.

'I suppose Deadly Nightshade had something to do with this,' said Harry. 'He's very keen on Tony; he's always looking at him.'

'So are other people!' said Ralph.

'Then of course they'll notice who's looking in the same direction,' said Michael.

'It's like the shepherd in Virgil, who had no chance with Alexis because he was the master's favourite,' said Harry.

'"*Formosum pastor Corydon ardebat Alexim Delicias domini*",' said Michael.

'Here he comes with Girlie,' said Ralph.

'I wondered if any of you chaps would care for an extra bathe?' said Dudley. 'Girling can round you up and bring you.'

He disappeared again.

'Come on, Staples,' said George.

'I don't care for an extra bathe,' said Harry. 'I'm not coming.'

'He refuses your invitation, with thanks,' said Ralph.

'I'm telling him to come, not inviting him.'

'On what authority?' asked Michael. 'Deadly Nightshade gave no order.'

'He expects him to come.'

'Then he'd better prepare himself for a disappointment,' said Ralph.

'You don't mind disappointing the Dud?' asked George.

'Not over much,' said Harry.

116

'I order you to come, as corporal of your patrol,' said George.

'I don't have to obey you,' said Harry. 'Guy is patrol leader.'

'In his absence I take his place,' said George.

'You don't, as we're not playing at Boy Scouts this afternoon, George,' said Ralph.

'Well, we'll see what comes of this,' said George.

'We'll wait and see,' said Harry, unperturbed.

'Really, Harry, it was too bad of you not to take the chance of an extra bathe this evening,' said Nan Hackett.

'I was asked if I would like to go,' said Harry. 'I was not ordered; it was an invitation.'

'We are sometimes expected to accept invitations,' said Nan. 'Ralph will tell you that; he strikes me as a boy who knows the world.'

'The world and school are two different things,' said Ralph. 'In the world, people haven't the same chance to give you orders.'

'And if one's invited, one has the freedom to refuse,' said Michael. 'Freedom is more important at school than in the world; one has so little. One mustn't waste it.'

'What a thing to say!' said Nan. 'You boys here strike me as having a great deal of freedom. What would the headmaster say?'

'I think he might say what we say,' said Michael. 'I don't know so much about Deadly Nightshade—oh, I beg your pardon, Miss Hackett—that was a slip. I meant Mr Knight.'

'I hope it was a slip, and that you didn't mean to be impertinent, Michael,' said Nan coldly. 'I know Mr Knight is always so friendly and simple with you all, so like a big boy himself, that he lets you call him "the Dud". But "Deadly Nightshade" is quite another thing

117

—it isn't a kind name, is it? So I shall put you all on your honour not to use it again.'

'Yes, Miss Hackett,' said Michael demurely.

'Deadly Nightshade looks a very big boy when he's dressed up as a scout,' said Ralph, a few minutes later. 'My mother would never let a man she knew appear in shorts if he had knees like that.'

'I thought Miss Hackett put us on our honour not to use that nickname for the Dud,' said George.

'I daresay she did,' said Hugh.

'Then don't you think it's rather rotten of you to do it, the moment her back's turned?'

'It would be very rude to do it to her face,' said Ralph.

'I don't think we made her any promise,' said Harry. 'I know I didn't.'

'It was only a schoolmistressy way of telling us not to do it,' said Michael.

'Didn't she put us on our scouts' honour?' said George.

'If she did, I don't think she had the right to,' said Ralph. 'She doesn't even dress up as a girl scout, like Miss Rigby.'

'Doesn't the Scout Law say that we have to obey masters and mistresses and all who are put in authority over us?'

'I think you've got it mixed up with the Catechism,' said Michael. 'But does it matter?'

'We swore to obey it,' said George.

'We had to,' said Harry. 'You're not obliged to keep promises that you've been forced to make.'

'No one made you,' said George. 'You could have refused to become a scout. Don't you remember what the Dud said on Empire Day about people withdrawing, if they didn't feel they could keep the promise?'

'If you think a boy can do what he likes about

118

becoming a scout in this school, George, you'd better think again,' said Ralph. 'That is, if you can think; which I should doubt.'

'It says in the prospectus that it's entirely voluntary,' said George.

'Mere hypocrisy,' said Harry. 'It goes on to say that every boy in the school joins—voluntary, my foot!'

'It's not entirely hypocrisy,' said Michael fairly. 'If our parents didn't want us to be scouts, we needn't; it's voluntary as far as they're concerned. We, of course, have no choice whatever.'

'Any way, I don't believe that we can take oaths that count until we're twenty-one,' said Ralph.

'What about our godfathers and godmothers in our baptism?' said George.

'What about them?' said someone.

'The Catechism says: "Dost thou not think thou art bound to do and perform what they then promised for thee?"'

'"Yea, verily, and by God's help so I will,"' said Tony, throwing a pillow at George.

'We're not bound because they promised, but because what they promised was right,' said Harry. 'We ought to forsake the Devil and all his works—including Deadly Nightshade.'

'If they'd promised we were to be Mohammedans, it would be our duty to break their promise,' said Michael.

'The Dud said that putting a boy on his honour is a solemn thing, like putting a soldier on parole,' said George, sticking up his nose.

'There's a difference,' said Harry. 'A prisoner of war gets an easier time if he's on parole: more freedom, and so on. If you put a soldier on parole, it's a bargain. But what do we gain by being put on our honour? It's no advantage to us that Miss Hackett isn't in the room, if we can't talk about Deadly Nightshade just as we like.'

'It's only an advantage to Miss Hackett,' said Ralph. 'She puts us on our honour, and then thinks she can go and woo Deadly Nightshade in the staff-room, and "the boys won't say anything they shouldn't".'

'There's no comparison,' said Michael. 'A soldier has to think about the other chaps on parole. Winston Churchill broke his parole and escaped, when he was a prisoner in the South African War; and the other chaps had a bad time because of him. My father said no gentleman ought to speak to him again.'

'It wouldn't make any difference to us if they didn't trust our "honour", as they call it,' said Harry.

'They don't trust us for a minute,' said Ralph. 'Don't let's talk as if they did. The stuff about "honour" is only to make us feel guilty. Deadly Nightshade trusts us less than any of them, because he thinks we're up to more wickedness than any of the others think.'

'By his standards, I suppose none of us are much good,' said George humbly.

'You've no idea how much worse he thinks us than we are,' said Ralph.

CHAPTER THIRTEEN

Dudley had invited Kit to take a turn with him on the terrace after supper.

'Christopher, dear boy,' he said suddenly. 'Tell me: what think you of Christ?'

'I should like to have notice of that question,' said Kit, showing great discomfort.

'No, Kit, don't run away,' said Dudley, gripping his arm, 'Let's just talk quietly for a while. After all, isn't it the most important subject in the world?'

'That must rather depend on what one's answer to the question is,' said Kit.

'Ah, yes,' said Dudley. 'You mean you must accept Him or reject Him, that there is no half-way course? He must be all or nothing?'

'I didn't quite mean that,' said Kit. 'He can't possibly be nothing; no one who has made so great a mark in world history could be that.'

'Then He must be everything,' said Dudley. 'The greatest Leader of men that the world has ever known....'

'Is He God?' said Kit. 'Everything surely hangs on that. I don't feel I yet know the answer to that question; and if that question is unanswered, then I can't know what to think of Him. The Prayer Book says He is; I think He said He was—but some people talked rather cagily in Ragstead chapel, and I'm not at all certain what you would say, either.'

'Oh, dear Christopher, I don't want to quarrel with

the grand old Prayer Book,' said Dudley. 'But some of us, in this modern age, are not so keen on dogmas and definitions and words like "consubstantial" that the plain man can't be expected to understand. Can't we be content to say that God was—is—undoubtedly in Him?'

'And in you and me, if God exists.'

'Undoubtedly.'

'I'm not at all content with a formula of that sort,' said Kit. 'It doesn't tell me what I want to know. Is He God, or is He a being merely of the same order as ourselves?'

'Isn't it enough for you that He is perfect man?'

'No,' said Kit. 'That seems to me just as dogmatic a statement as any other that is made about Him—and why should I follow any other man, however good?'

'Oh, Christopher! But when you read of His wonderful sayings and doings, you must feel: "Here is the example I ought to copy." '

'Not always,' said Kit. 'Often I couldn't copy; there are things I couldn't do. I can't turn water into wine or walk on the sea. I couldn't feed the whole school—much less Five Thousand people—with a few loaves and fishes.'

'I wonder how literally we are meant to take those beautiful old stories,' said Dudley. 'Isn't it enough to suppose that the simple people who were with Him felt they were refreshed?'

'Can we pick and choose what we are to believe?' said Kit. 'It all comes to us on the same authority. Mustn't we either believe everything or nothing?'

'That's a dangerous line to take,' said Dudley. 'It might lead you to atheism—or even to Rome. No, just think of the beautiful and obviously true things that you can't help accepting. Dear boy, I respect your honest doubt, and I am glad you feel you can confide in me like this. All will straighten itself out, believe me: Just try to do, as a friend of mine did: give as much of yourself as you can to as much of Christ as you know.'

'There are too many other difficulties,' said Kit.

'Ah, I know,' said Dudley, squeezing his arm.

'I did not mean personal difficulties,' said Kit, coldly. 'If Christ is God, He's above criticism: what He did or said must necessarily be right. They might be things that a human being neither could nor should do. I don't worry that He did things that I find unattractive: that He cursed the barren fig-tree, or flogged the money-changers, or told men to believe in Him or to follow Him. He acted as God, or as a bad man—*aut Deus aut homo non bonus*.'

'That weird mediaeval formula!' said Dudley. 'Does it satisfy you?'

'You must correct me if I am wrong,' said Kit, 'I thought it was patristic. No, I can see a third possibility. He may have been neither God nor a conscious impostor, but a good and even a great man with a single delusion.'

'So you turn away from Him, Christopher?' said Dudley sorrowfully.

'No,' said Kit. 'I wait for certainty, one way or the other. I may never get it, but till I do I can't take sides. I can't bet on it, as Pascal would like me to do. Of course I wouldn't let the boys suspect this but, as you know, the only Scripture I do with them is Old Testament history.'

'There's a bit too much of that, here,' said Dudley. 'You might mention it to your good uncle that religious instruction doesn't consist in learning lists of the kings of Israel and Judah.'

'I'm a temporary,' said Kit. 'I don't like to interfere.'

'Sad it is that you leave us so soon, dear boy,' said Dudley. 'I admire your honesty, and hope you will find an answer to your question—unless, indeed, you come to drop your question, and just to follow Christ—the carpenter with or without the halo.'

'He would be no good to me without the halo,' said Kit. 'If it was just man for man, I might like Socrates better.'

'You can't really mean that, Christopher,' said Dudley.

'I certainly do,' said Kit. 'I find the Greek world so much more attractive than Judaea any way. Of course, if Christ is God, that is another thing; then He is to be worshipped, on one's knees and with incense. I don't want a man to imitate or follow.'

'I don't quite know what to say to you,' said Dudley. 'Of course, as a padre ...'

'Are you a padre? Are you a priest, Father Knight?' said Kit. 'Have you an awful power given to you to cast out devils and to forgive sins, and to offer sacrifice for the quick and the dead?'

'I am in priest's orders,' said Dudley. 'But I don't care for the word very much—and as for these "awful powers", I prefer to dwell on other sides of my calling. I should say I had a humble commission to point the way, to be a "sky-pilot", as they say.'

'I don't like that word any more than you like the word "priest".' said Kit. 'I should not go for advice to anyone of your cloth, except as a priest.'

'Then I am almost inclined to hope you will go on by your own light,' said Dudley. 'I am sure it will be given to you, dear boy.'

Dudley wandered again by the edge of the cricket-field and called boys from the pursuit of butterflies or the search for four-leaved clover to go to the swimming-bath.

Harry Staples could, for once, feel glad that he was fielding, and that he was secure from such an invitation.

Unexpectedly Dudley came up to him at his post at long-stop.

'You're not doing much here, Staples,' he said. 'Won't you come for a bathe?'

'I'm fielding, sir,' said Harry.

Dudley fixed on him those eyes which he knew by experience to be hypnotic, and cooed: 'Won't you come? I'll let you off the rest of the game.'

'If I must,' said Harry, in resignation.

'There is no must,' said Dudley.

'Then I would rather not, thank you, sir,' said Harry.

Dudley gave him a sorrowful look, and then it was the end of the over, and Harry had some way to walk.

At the other side of the field he encountered Nan Hackett, who was deputizing for Matron in the care of bruises.

'So, you have let him down again?' she said. 'How can you be so stubborn and unkind? Don't you know it was largely for you that he took the trouble to come down this evening? Will you throw away one opportunity after another?'

Her voice clogged with emotion. She took him by the shoulder in no gentle grip, and said; 'Run! You still have a chance to catch up with the others. If you don't take it, I give you up!'

Harry paused for a moment. 'Very well, Miss Hackett,' he said, and left the field.

Up at the swimming-bath he at once repented his decision, for none of his particular friends was there; they were still fielding. There seemed, however, to be no one in charge, so there was no reason why he should not leave at once if he chose. He decided to do this.

Kit came out of the pavilion, and saw that a number of boys were absent.

'Mr Knight took them for a bathe,' said Nan.

'Where is Harry?' asked Kit, after a few minutes. 'I thought he was fielding.'

'He's gone to the swimming-bath,' said Nan.

'Did Mr Knight tell him to go?' asked Kit in surprise.

'No,' said Nan. 'But I felt sure he must be very disappointed when Harry didn't take his chance. It was more than I could bear; I urged him to go.'

'It's more than I can bear to think of Harry having to go,' said Kit. 'I suppose Mr Knight is there in charge?'

'I don't know,' said Nan.

'Once before he let them go by themselves,' said Kit. 'I can't let Harry be there without a master present. Will you take charge here for a few minutes, Miss Hackett?'

'You're on duty here, Mr Henderson,' said Nan stiffly.

'I'm baths master,' said Kit. 'I'm responsible if the bath is being used.'

'Don't you think you can safely leave that to Mr Knight? After all, in his senior position...'

'I daresay he did not even know that Harry was going,' said Kit. 'He may just have unlocked the gate, and let the boys go in. He's done that once before.'

'Well, what harm can happen?' said Nan.

'There may be bullying,' said Kit. 'And nothing can happen on the cricket field, if you are here.'

'A boy might be killed by a ball.'

'Well, I couldn't prevent that any more than you,' said Kit. 'It has happened, I know; I often think cricket should be suppressed, myself...'

'You're trying to shock me, Mr Henderson,' said Nan with a disagreeable smile. 'You can't do that quite so easily. But I do wish you wouldn't make that sort of remark; it may make you enemies.'

'I am afraid I must run,' said Kit, and he did so.

He was in time to find George Girling gripping Harry

126

by the wrists, while Ronald Gibson was pulling off his clothes. Harry was wriggling and squirming, and trying to get his teeth into George's ear. None of the other boys was taking any part in the struggle; some were swimming, and others were looking on.

Kit, in cold anger, seized the pole to which the belt was attached, and thrust it hard at George, who released Harry and fell upon the grass, letting out howls of pain.

'I'm afraid you've injured him seriously, sir,' said Ronald Gibson, hopping round him maliciously. 'You hit him hard between the legs, you know.'

'Serve him right, young brute!' said Kit. 'And I shall report you too, Ronald, to the headmaster. I won't stand for bullying.'

'Mr Knight, sir, said he'd always punish the boy who was being bullied most,' said Ronald. 'You wouldn't want Harry to be punished, would you?'

'If Harry deserved punishment, I should not interfere to save him,' said Kit coldly. 'I don't know what Mr Knight would do, but I think I know very well what Mr Langton will. You and George will be thrashed within an inch of your lives.'

'I doubt if George's health can stand it sir, after what you've done to him,' said Ronald.

Dudley again sought a conference in the headmaster's study.

'It was unwise of Christopher to hit a boy,' he said gravely. 'We have always left corporal punishment to the headmaster of this school.'

'I was not punishing that young thug; I hope he has that coming to him from my uncle,' said Kit. 'I was interfering between him and his victim. It wouldn't have been necessary, if you hadn't left them unattended in the swimming-bath.'

'Yes, Knight,' said the headmaster. 'That must not occur again.'

'Oh, it was only a little horse-play, Girling told me,' said Dudley.

'Very cruel horse-play,' said Kit. 'Harry Staples told me they were pulling off his clothes, and meant to throw him in. He'd let Miss Hackett persuade him to go for a bathe. When he found no master in attendance he very wisely decided to go away, as none of his friends were here—then these little swine set on him.'

'Do you know they would have thrown him in?' said Dudley. 'Girling and Gibson say it was only fun.'

'Of course they would,' said Kit. 'At all events, Harry thought he was going to be thrown in—and that was enough for me. I had to stop it.'

'You might easily have done Girling a serious injury,' Dudley dropped his voice. 'You might have prevented him from ever becoming a father.'

'Well, he can't be thinking of that just yet,' said Langton with a laugh. 'Though if he stays at school till he can do quadratic equations, he may be a grandfather first.'

'He's not the sort one wants to breed from,' said Kit.

'It would have done the school untold harm,' hissed Dudley.

'Well, I suppose if Harry had had a bad nervous breakdown, it would be no advertisement for us either,' said Kit.

'Christopher, I think you're in danger of being taken in by that boy, Staples,' said Dudley. 'Do you really believe the other fellows would have stood aside, and let him be tormented to that extent? Don't you think some of them would have rushed to his defence, if his story is true?'

'No, I don't,' said Kit. 'I think they could have killed him without anyone trying to stop them.'

128

'That's what you think of the spirit of this school!'
said Dudley.

'It's no worse than that of any other,' said Kit. 'Surely
only women believe in those romantic school stories
about the hero punishing the bully? I imagine they
write them.'

'Of course,' said Langton. 'You know that as well as I
do, Knight. Only authority can stop bullying; other boys
can't and won't. Small boys are not bullied by big boys,
because they are kept apart from them; we see to that.
Boys are bullied by other boys of their own age, two or
three against one.'

'It's just as well that the other boys keep out of it,'
said Kit. 'One doesn't want a free fight.'

'A pity journalists and parsons draw that precious
analogy from their ignorance of school life, and tell us to
make war in defence of the small nations,' said Langton.

'I think St Augustine started it,' said Dudley. 'Of
course he was a parson, like myself.'

'Then I hope he confessed it in his *Confessions*,' said
Langton. 'It's one of the most mischievous pieces of false
reasoning that ever took people in.'

'I still don't understand the situation at all,' said Kit
to Dudley. 'I can't understand how you or Nan Hackett
let Harry Staples go for an extra bathe. I thought my
uncle had decided that he was not to be bothered any
more about swimming, and that he was just to go in for
a formal dip in the morning.'

'You gave no orders of any sort, Headmaster,' said
Dudley. 'I heard of none.'

'Kit is quite right, those were my instructions for the
morning bathe. Kit and Matron are in charge, and they
knew all about them; there was no need for anyone else
to be told. I'd never thought about these irregular
evening bathes. If they happen again, Harry is not to go.

He was a fool to let Nan persuade him, and she was a fool too. I shall speak to her severely.'

'I suppose she thought he might have made an effort when the bath was nearly empty, and that his friends might have helped him,' said Dudley feebly.

'Instead of which his enemies have scared him out of his wits,' said Kit. 'I hoped he might learn to swim quietly in the holidays: now it's obvious that he must leave it alone for years.'

CHAPTER FOURTEEN

The headmaster allowed himself to be persuaded that, in view of Kit's attack upon him, George Girling should be let off with a severe rebuke; it was therefore impossible to inflict any further punishment on his accomplice, Ronald Gibson. Nevertheless, the rebuke was as severe as it could be, and George came from it to the Grey Room with flushed nose and red eyes. He felt that he had been ill-treated, and Ronald, as usual, was vindictive.

'You were a sneak to tell Henderson that we were going to throw you in!' said George.

'He could see for himself,' said Harry. 'He didn't need telling.'

'You could have told him it was a joke,' said George.

'I never thought of that,' said Harry sarcastically.

'It was no joke for Harry,' said Ralph Wimbush.

'I don't see why Harry should tell lies to save you and Ronald,' said Michael Park.

'What about Hubert Tracy, who died rather than sneak?' said George.

This was a school legend. Guy Tracy's younger brother had in fact died at school a year previously from an internal injury. No one knew how it had been caused, nor if another boy had caused it. There was no reason to suppose that he would have recovered had all been known.

'More fool he!' said Ralph and Harry together.

'If that was really how it was,' said Michael. 'But I don't believe it for a moment.'

George appeared deeply shocked. 'I'll tell Guy what you said,' he said to Ralph and Harry. 'He'll be very angry.'

'He'll be very angry with you,' said Tony. 'If you say anything to him about it, I'll punch your nose hard enough to squash all the fleas in it.'

'And I suppose you wouldn't call telling Guy "sneaking",' said Michael with contempt.

'He ought to know what people are saying about his dead brother,' said George, lifting his nose.

'He oughtn't,' said Tony. 'He can't bear talking about Hubert.'

Nan Hackett came in, to make a routine visit.

'What's all the gossip about?' she asked.

'Harry and Ralph were saying that Hubert Tracy was a fool,' said George.

'You shouldn't speak ill of the dead,' said Nan.

'We weren't,' said Ralph. 'George believes the ridiculous story that he died rather than tell who hurt him.'

'And we said he would have been a fool if he did,' said Harry. 'And so he would.'

'I should hardly expect either of you to understand loyalty,' said Nan, who was still smarting from the rebuke that she had received on Harry's account. 'You've neither of you ever shown much sign of it.'

'Just as well,' said Ralph, as she went out of the room. 'If that's what she means.'

' "Loyalty" is just another schoolmistressy word,' said Michael. 'It means putting up with any nonsense from our elders and betters and never saying a word about it.'

' "My Dudley, right or wrong!" ' said Ralph.

'The only person who has shown real loyalty is Tony,' said Michael. 'He has stuck up for Guy behind his back,

132

and has told George to keep his horrid nose out of his affairs.'

'And we've been loyal to ourselves, though George tried to sneak to Nan,' said Ralph.

'We'll get our own back one day, you'll see,' said Ronald.

On Sunday they walked through the fields to the village church; the boys wore Eton suits and straw hats. Those in authority tried to instil into them some respect for the day and for their clothes; they were discouraged from wading in a marsh to pick wild irises, or from lingering by a pond to watch the amorous play of ducks.

Michael was walking with Guy and Tony, who might have been dragged asunder and assigned to uncongenial partners had they not had a third person with them. Michael was helping Tony to prepare Guy for possible impertinence.

'Thank you,' said Guy. 'I quite see how it was. I don't mind talking to friends about Hubert. But I shall shut up George pretty quickly; and if Nan tries to start anything I shall go at once to Dick and Mary.'

Harry and Ralph were walking together. Harry was to be called for after church by Lady Best-Pennant. He had been asked to luncheon at the Towers with Dudley and 'one other boy', and Ralph had been good-natured enough to consent to go.

'It will be pretty grim,' Harry warned him.

'I like seeing houses and people,' said Ralph. 'And I can help you to keep an eye on Deadly Nightshade; it might be amusing.'

They sat in the Hazelcroft pews in front of the church, two decorous rows of boys in black jackets and white collars. Their singing was supposed to encourage the congregation.

Round the Lord, in glory seated,
Cherubim and Seraphim...

Ralph and Harry waited in Lady Best-Pennant's motor for Dudley, who had helped the vicar with the service, and had gone to disrobe in the vestry.

'He'll have to call us by our Christian names for once,' said Ralph. 'You, at least, in your aunt's house.'

'He'll do it in an unnatural sort of way,' said Harry. 'As if he wasn't used to it—and of course he isn't.'

The Towers, which had but one etiolated tower, was a large, hideous house built during the previous reign. Inside it was spacious and draughty, and full of oriental objects in expensive bad taste.

'What a privilege for you to spend your holidays in this beautiful home!' said Dudley to Harry, as the motor-car stopped in the sweep, surrounded by dark evergreens.

'A welcome change from school grub, eh boys!' he said heartily, as they sat down to luncheon.

Plates of rather scraggy mutton were put in front of them, and a footman handed two depressing vegetable dishes.

'Of course it is a pleasure to see Lady Best-Pennant and her house,' said Ralph politely. 'But we mustn't give her the idea that we don't have good food at school.' He turned over a cabbage stalk with distaste.

'It is nice to hear boys loyal to their school,' said their hostess with approval.

Dudley looked displeased at such praise of Ralph, but he soon adjusted his tone.

'Perhaps boys are too well looked after at school nowadays,' he said. 'I know when I was at school what a treat it would have been to go out to a good meal.' And he paused, to dislodge a piece of gristle from a front tooth. 'It seems almost unnatural for boys not to complain of school food,' he said. 'I remember end of term rhymes:

> *No more tadpoles in the tea*
> *Making silly eyes at me . . . .'*

Lady Best-Pennant forced a polite smile.

Dudley asked how she was going to spend the summer, and learned that she intended to visit an Austrian spa.

'And what are young Harry's plans?'

'I understand he is to go to his cousins—my step-daughters, in the Isle of Wight,' she replied stiffly.

Dudley then brought out his plan for a holiday tutor. The young man could find lodgings near by, and need be no bother to the ladies. Harry could meet him in the morning, first thing, for a bathe; then, after breakfast, there might be a little boxing, and a second bathe before lunch. Some afternoons could be left free for excursions or other social activities; on others there could be nets for cricket.

'It would not be much of a holiday,' said Ralph boldly.

'Some boys would love it, I suppose,' said Lady Best-Pennant. 'What do you say, Harry?'

'I would rather stay at school,' said Harry. 'There would be no point in going away to a holiday like that.'

'No point in going to your cousins, Harry?' said Dudley reproachfully. 'You should be more polite; remember that they are your aunt's step-daughters.'

'There would be no pleasure in seeing anyone in a life like that,' said Harry. 'And my cousins would only be unhappy if they saw me having to do all these things.'

'I am afraid that is perhaps true,' said his aunt.

'What would the boy's father think?' asked Dudley.

'One does feel that Harry is a boy who needs some special preparation for public school life, if he is to get out of it and give to it all that he should. A man would see that.'

'There would just be time to write to the Colonel, I suppose,' said Lady Best-Pennant. 'I don't quite know what my nephew—it seems absurd to call him my nephew—would say.'

'Absurd indeed!' said Dudley gushingly.

'I doubt if the Colonel would care for the expense, unless he were sure that the boy himself wished it,' she said in an honest tone.

'Then we must unite, you and I, Lady Best-Pennant, in an appeal to young Harry. We must ask him to think of his own best interests and to write to his good father. I feel sure we can prevail on him.'

'Not with me here, sir,' said Ralph. 'He is not defenceless.'

'Wimbush, that is a very uncalled for remark, Ralph,' said Dudley. 'I don't know what our hostess can think of your manners.'

'I think he is a brave boy, Mr Knight,' said Lady Best-Pennant. 'Harry is lucky to have so good a friend.'

'I shall not sign my own death-warrant,' said Harry, emboldened by the turn things were taking.

'It's another year and more before Harry goes to a public school,' said his aunt. 'There's no need to hurry things. He may develop by himself without all this expense.'

'I might die first,' said Harry. 'Then all that misery would have been wasted.'

'Or the public school system might come to an end,' said Ralph. 'Or it might be very much reformed. People often attack it in the newspapers.'

'We will venture to hope that neither of these things will occur,' said Dudley. 'And I think you will find that those who speak or write against the public schools belong to two classes of people: those who are envious, because they have not been to a public school, and those who are spiteful, because they made a failure of their public school life—the best life in the world.'

'It must be fine training,' said Lady Best-Pennant.

'But life begins when school is over, so Mr Henderson says,' said Ralph.

'They have a very bright young master this term,' Dudley explained. 'He is almost too clever and modern for old stagers like me.'

'Oh, Mr Knight!' protested their hostess.

'He sharpens the boys' wits,' said Dudley. 'Sometimes I wonder if they're not a little too sharp for their age.'

'I shall like to meet him, when I come over for the Sports. Or for the play at Christmas.'

'Oh, he'll be gone by then,' said Dudley cheerfully.

'You mean—he is not fitting in with the school?'

'No, no,' said Dudley. 'But he's only a temporary. He goes up to Cambridge in the autumn.'

'I wish he was here for good,' said Harry.

'Yes, he has an appeal for some of the boys,' said Dudley. 'And I shall be sorry to see the last of young Henderson.'

Lady Best-Pennant said firmly that the boys would like to play in the garden until tea. It was her own custom to rest, and she offered Dudley the choice of the library or the smoking-room; he said that he did not smoke, and chose the former.

'He could equally truly have said that he doesn't read,' said Harry, 'but I suppose he wouldn't like to admit it.'

'Your aunt didn't invite him to share her rest,' said Ralph. 'I don't think there's much danger of his becoming your uncle.'

'Dudley might like someone younger than Aunt Hilda, after all.'

'Probably,' said Ralph. 'But that's not all. I beg your pardon, Harry, because, as Mother says, nothing annoys people more than speaking well of their relations. . . .'

'You don't mean you like Aunt Hilda?'

'I wouldn't go quite so far as that,' said Ralph. 'The woman has a monstrous house, and food that's practically uneatable; but she's too straightforward for Dudley. I don't think she likes him very much. I'm sure she wouldn't join in any of his plots and plans.'

'No, I believe you're right,' said Harry.

'You saw how she dealt with him at luncheon,' said Ralph. 'You needn't fear that she will ever be in league with him against you. You'll never have that dreadful young man punching you about in the holidays.'

'She doesn't like me,' said Harry.

'Why should she?' said Ralph. 'You don't like her at all. But she'll be fair to you. She'll consider your rights. While Nan might like you—and I daresay she thinks she does—but she'd cut you into little pieces if she thought it would do her any good with Deadly Nightshade.'

'I don't think Nan knows the difference between right and wrong,' said Harry. 'People like her, who think themselves rather good, often don't.'

'Your aunt may be a beast to your cousins, but I expect she's a just beast.'

'Perhaps,' said Harry grudgingly.

'I don't think she cares for Deadly Nightshade at all,' said Ralph. 'But, as she's a foreigner, he has one advantage with her. She mightn't notice that he's not a gentleman.'

'And as she's a foreigner, can we be sure if she's a lady?'

'We'll ask my mother on Sports Day,' said Ralph.

Dudley, warmed by tea, was in a genial mood as the Daimler carried them back to Hazelcroft.

'Well, this is a grand way to be returning to school!' he said, forgetting that such a means of transport was familiar to both the boys.

'A Daimler is all right for a short drive, sir,' said Ralph. 'But I must say that on the whole I prefer a Rolls.'

'We're not all so grand as you!' said Dudley, and almost without malice.

'And now, Harry Staples,' he continued. 'I hope you regret making up those ridiculous stories about the kind lady who has so hospitably entertained us, for we see how baseless they are.'

'I didn't make up any stories,' said Harry. 'I told Ralph some things my cousins told me, and Ronald Gibson and George Girling added to them.'

'Now, no tales out of school,' said Dudley. 'We won't mention the matter again. I said nothing to your good aunt.'

'Why "no tales out of school"?' said Harry, when he was alone with Ralph. 'It's one of the silliest things people say. I thought it was in school that one shouldn't tell tales; I wish George and Ronald would learn that.'

'And I don't see how our visit to the Towers proves anything,' said Ralph. 'There weren't tins of weed-killer about; you wouldn't expect it. But that disgusting trifle did give me an idea. Lady Best-Pennant could easily have poisoned your uncle by accident with her horrible food.'

CHAPTER FIFTEEN

It was Sports Day; the boys had a picnic luncheon on the sunk lawn. Matron and Nan presided over the distribution of hard-boiled eggs, of tomatoes and sausage rolls. Ginger-beer bottles popped with a festive air, and there was a feeling of holiday.

In the dining-room invited (or self-invited) parents were being entertained by the Langtons and by Dudley Knight. Cold hams had been sliced and cold chickens cut up in the kitchen; there were great bowls of salad, trifles thickly coated with cream, and vast raspberry and red currant tarts. There were enormous frosted jugs of cider-cup in which strawberries and bits of cucumber floated.

From the sunk lawn the boys could see upwards on to the gravel sweep, where cars were arriving.

'Isn't that George Girling's parents?' asked someone.

'No, I bet they're inside, guzzling,' said Michael Park. 'Catch any of that family not taking the chance of a free meal—and probably a very good one too.'

'They may have been asked,' said Tony Stuart. 'After all, they must count among the better sort of parents. He's a Brigadier.'

'The awful Gibsons are in there,' said Ralph Wimbush. 'Taking advantage of being neighbours. Just the sort of thing one should not do—they could come at any time.'

'My Aunt Hilda is coming over in the afternoon,' said Harry.

'Much better taste,' said Ralph.

'And what on earth can they do all the time after luncheon?' said Guy.

'They'll look at the "dear boys" and make a nuisance of themselves,' said Michael. 'And Dick will have to keep his temper with them; and we shall pay for it tomorrow.'

Sure enough, Mrs Langton came into the play-room with a mother, and the boys leapt to their feet, as if a rude hand had snatched them from their brief refuge in Anthony Hope or Rider Haggard or Dumas.

Harry Staples, more deeply absorbed in his reading, was a little late in rising, but he rose, reluctantly, to his feet, with a finger in his book.

'A shame to disturb them!' said the mother, having done so.

'You were deliberately rude to Tom Smith-Ramsbotham's mater,' said George Girling accusingly.

'Oh, stow it, Girlie,' said Michael Park.

'What the Hell's it got to do with you?' said Ralph Wimbush.

'It's everyone's business that the school should be known for its good manners,' said George, pompously.

'I suppose you think you're an advertisement for it?' said Michael Park. 'Because you'd win the prize for the biggest cabbage grown in the human nose.'

The heats had already taken place on previous days, and only the finals of the running and jumping were to be decided.

'I'm so glad Guy's won,' said Canon Stuart.

'Your wife's not here, Archdeacon?' said Mrs Stuart.

'She can't bring herself to come here; because of Hubert, you know, our second boy,' said the Archdeacon. 'Not that the school was to blame. It was one of those inexplicable, horrifying things that occur.'

Mrs Stuart made a sound of sympathy, having no words.

'It's good of you to let us have Tony for part of the holidays,' said the Archdeacon. 'It will make things better for Guy.'

'But harder for your wife, I'm afraid,' said Mrs Stuart gently. 'It's very noble of her to welcome him.'

'If she sees Guy happier, she'll be well rewarded,' said the Archdeacon.

'Is that the Earl of Barchester?' said Mrs Girling to Mrs Stuart, with great interest.

The Canon seized the opportunity to take the Archdeacon aside.

'Has that ghastly fellow Knight said anything impertinent to you?' he asked. 'I thought he was very offensive to me about our boys—thought they were too thick. I told him off, I can tell you.'

'I don't think he'd quite dare to say anything of the sort to me,' said the Archdeacon. 'He knows Guy has lost his brother.'

'There's something not quite right about that man,' said the Canon. 'He's all mixed up. And I believe he doesn't exercise his orders—never celebrates Holy Communion.'

'That always looks fishy,' said the Archdeacon. 'The school will be all right as long as old Langton stays, but it will go to pot when he retires.'

'My dear, what fun hurdles are!' said Mrs Wimbush. 'But it must be horrid to bark one's shins on them.'

'Someone seems to have retired hurt,' said Bill Barchester.

'Good, it's George Girling,' said Ralph vindictively.

'Oh, my dear, wasn't that the boy who made the divine *mot* about my being in "seduced circumstances"?' said Charlotte.

''Sh, that's his mother,' said Ralph.

'Oh, Mrs Wimbush, haven't we met here before?' said Mrs Girling. 'And isn't that the Earl with you?'

'Bill? I suppose he is one,' said Charlotte Wimbush, and introduced them.

Presently she called him back. 'Bill, darling, did I ever tell you how perfectly Ralph has planned all his little friends' futures and his own?' she said. 'You and I are to guarantee his social success at Eton; Michael Park and Harry Staples are to be intellectuals; that Girling boy is to make his way as a tough, and that sweet Tony Stuart is to be a tart!'

'Charlotte, my dear, *pas devant l'enfant, pas devant!*' said Bill Barchester.

'The Girling boy is crying,' said Mrs Wimbush. 'Perhaps he won't even make his way as a tough; what do you think, Mr Henderson?' For Kit had come up, and was grinning at her remarks.

'Poor lad, I'm not sure if he'll succeed in that short and glorious career,' said Kit. 'Sad to become an "old boy" at eighteen, and to live on the past for ever after, while the moths eat one's coloured scarves and sweaters.'

'Ralph's chosen better for himself,' said Mrs Wimbush with a laugh. 'The English will always love a lord, won't they Bill? And though he won't be the rose, Ralph will always be near the rose.'

'And Michael and Harry will come into their own with their brains, about the time George is finished,' said Kit, with satisfaction.

'And Tony will only be beginning to look his best!' said Mrs Wimbush. 'He'll be divine at eighteen!'

'Cradle-snatcher!' said Lord Barchester fondly.

'That's what I shall have come to by that time,' said Charlotte, with a sigh.

'The headmaster's getting on,' said one father to another. 'Soon be past the job.'

'Knight will take on,' said the other. 'Active feller. Never lets the boys slack off on discipline.'

'When I heard the boys weren't allowed to put their hands in their pockets, that was enough for me,' said the first father. 'I put my little lad down for the school at once, though he was only three.'

'A fine sight, Mrs Langton,' said a parent. 'I suppose this is your great day in the year?'

'It's the day we're on show,' said Mary Langton. 'But I suppose it's really the least important day; it's not a day when much education goes on.'

'Oh, education,' said Colonel Gibson. 'I think the ancient Persians were pretty sound about it; just teach a boy to ride and shoot and speak the truth.'

'There are some boys whom one could never teach to speak the truth,' said Mary, and bit her lip as she remembered that Ronald was one of them.

Anita Rigby was changing her place to get a better view of the long jump, and Mary pounced on her eagerly.

'This is Colonel Gibson, Miss Rigby; I don't think you've met, and of course you should. Isn't Ronald your prize pupil?'

'He's doing well,' said Miss Rigby, with an approximation to truthfulness. 'It's his friend, George Girling, who's really my most promising artist.'

'Miss Rigby teaches music,' said Mr Langton. 'She is also our art teacher.'

'Well, I care a lot for naychah'—said Colonel Gibson, clearing his throat, as if he were about to make an important or interesting statement. 'And I never feel art comes up to naychah.'

'Colonel Gibson, isn't it? I know how kind you've been to George,' said Mrs Girling. 'Come over here and talk to the Earl,' she added, as if she were making a return for his hospitality.

144

But Bill Barchester and Charlotte Wimbush had walked off to a trestle table, where Peggy was dispensing iced coffee and iced lemonade. They might help themselves to cress or cucumber sandwiches.

Ralph hovered in attendance.

'Darling, what's the name of that nice, obviously pregnant maid?' asked Mrs Wimbush.

'Hush, my dear!' said Bill Barchester. *'Pas devant!'*

'Ow, Mrs Wimbush and the Earl of Barchester; well met!' said an enthusiastic but common voice, that of Mrs Gibson.

'Dear Mrs Gibson!' said Charlotte sweetly. 'You who live in the neighbourhood, reassure me. Do our poor little sons get anything like the delicious grub that we bloated parents are given on these grand occasions?'

'My boy says the food's much better than it is at home,' said Mrs Gibson. 'That's his fun, of course.'

'Shouldn't wonder if it was true,' muttered Bill Barchester. 'Don't like the look of that woman, not wholesome; complexion like mortadella.'

'There's Harry's German aunt,' said George Girling, who had recovered from his mishap at the hurdles. He said it to Ronald Gibson, but his voice carried.

'Partly German, and his great-aunt-by-marriage,' said Lady Best-Pennant in a clear voice, as she passed on her way.

'Oh, cripes!' cried Ronald, doubled up with laughter.

'Stow it, you ass!' said George Girling, in an agony of fear. 'Suppose she tells the Dud?'

'She's sure to do that, as they're such friends,' said Ronald with enjoyment.

'My God, what can I do?' said George. 'Shall I run after her and apologize?'

'That would only make it worse,' said Ronald.

'Shall I get hold of Harry, and ask him to beg her not to mention it?' said George desperately.

'I shouldn't think Harry would do anything for you,' said Ronald. 'And this wouldn't be an easy thing to do.'

'She may say nothing, as she doesn't know my name,' George tried to console himself.

'She'll say "the boy with the nose",' said Ronald. 'But I should think you'll get off with nothing worse than a severe rebuke.'

'But the Dud won't trust me any more!' said George with a sob.

'You seem to be always crying this afternoon, George,' said Nan Hackett. 'I shall tell Mr Knight that I can't think why he calls you such a brave boy.'

George sobbed the more.

'Would you like me to find your mother for you?' said Nan unkindly.

There was a stir and bustle. The athletic events were over, and now there were to be what Mr Langton called the 'bumblepuppy races'.

'Lowbrow of me,' said Mrs Wimbush to someone. 'But they're the only things that amuse me; and one's boy is in them, of course.'

Ralph and his clever friends were indeed taking part in the sack race, the egg and spoon race and the three-legged race. The headmaster expected boys to take some part in the sports, and these games amused them; they had paid their tribute to pure athletics by entering for the hundred yards (which was less trouble than anything else) and none of them had been left in for the finals.

'God, what a beautiful face!' exclaimed Mrs Wimbush. 'I mean the boy who's just won the sack race.'

'What, Michael Park!' said Kit in surprise. 'But I see what you mean.'

The young head projecting from the sack, with tangled hair, and brilliant with colour and amusement and the pleasure of winning, was unlike that which he saw daily in class.

146

'He's intelligent, of course,' said Kit.

'You have to be intelligent to win these races,' said Mrs Wimbush. 'Any lout can run or jump.'

Now it was the three-legged race. 'So symbolical!' said Mrs Wimbush, turning to Dudley Knight. 'It's how one's got to stumble through life, isn't it, tied to a husband or a lover? Violently difficult not to get tied up in knots or to collapse; and such a danger of hurting oneself or one's partner.'

'You've given me a new thought,' said Dudley, with an attempt at joviality. 'I shall use it next time I'm asked to give an address at a wedding. You're right, you know; slow and steady wins the race, and keeping in step.'

'Yes, try to cut a dash, and you're both on the ground, and wriggling to get loose,' said Mrs Wimbush, with a sigh. 'At first one really wanted to be tied to a lover (extraordinary as it seems afterwards). I wonder if the boys feel like that; but I suppose they're too young still.'

'Let us hope so,' said Bill Barchester repressively, before Dudley Knight had time to find words.

'There's Ralph, with good little Harry Staples,' went on Mrs Wimbush. 'That's obviously not a love match, but I shouldn't be a bit surprised if they won. They've probably practised. Ralph's very efficient.'

They did win.

And now the bishop was asked to give away the prizes.

'That's very grand, for a prep school,' said one parent. 'How did they get hold of him?'

'I don't think it's the bishop of the diocese,' said someone else. 'Just a suffragan.'

There he stood, a stout handsome man in a purple cassock, twiddling his pectoral cross.

'Sometimes I find myself at school prize-givings,' he said, 'on a platform between a lady holding a huge bouquet of flowers, and a politician or a military man.

The politician or the military man speaks first, and very often he tells the audience that he has never got a prize at school—and I must say, from the look of him, and from his speech, I should guess that he was telling the truth. Then everyone claps wildly, and laughs—I suppose that is what he means them to do, but I often wonder if it is really polite—and the poor boys look almost ashamed when they come up to receive their prizes.

'Well, dear boys, from looking at me, you'd guess that I'd never won a prize in any school sports, wouldn't you? And you'd be perfectly right. I *was* once runner-up for the egg and spoon race, and but for a foul on the part of the winner I should have got the prize—but he's an archbishop now, so we'll let byegones be byegones.

'All the same, it's nice to be good at something—I don't know that it matters very much what it is—but it does a boy good to be able to write Latin verses or to do the Long Jump better than his neighbour; to be quicker at running or at mental arithmetic. I approve of prize-winners, and I applaud them.

'At this stage, the politician or the military man, whom I so often listen to (or pretend to listen to) at prize-givings, would try to make the winners feel thoroughly uncomfortable by saying that many of the best men, like themselves, had never won a prize, as a sort of pat on the back to the boys who had won nothing.

'Have I a pat on the back, you may ask, to give to those who have never won a prize? I have, but first I congratulate the prize-winners; for it is their day today; and I hope they will win prizes of all kinds in the future too.

'This brings me to my point; there are prizes of all kinds to be won in life. Even in an excellent school like this there are no prizes given for a lot of activities that are only hobbies now, but one day may carry some of you much further than Latin Prose or the High Jump.

Music, photography, plant-collecting, dancing, acting—
all the arts and sciences, in short. For many of you your
prizes may, perhaps, be coming later. But at least try,
from now onwards, to excel in something; to rise at
least in one thing above the common herd and the dull
average.'

'Rotten feller,' said Brigadier Girling to Colonel
Gibson. 'Very bad taste, that, about politicians and
military men. Who does he think he is? He'll never be
more than a suffragan; I hear he's a socialist.'

Disentangling his pince-nez from his pectoral cross,
the bishop was trying to read the list that had been
handed to him.

'High Jump: Guy Bracy.'

'Tracy, my Lord,' said someone at his elbow.

'The common herd, the dull average!' exclaimed
Dudley in indignation to one of his admirers among the
parents. 'What a thing to say to boys who are here to
learn the team-spirit, which is the central message of the
public schools, and the keynote of democracy!'

'Hundred yards, Hugh Tup, Tup, what's this?'

'Tupholme, my Lord.'

'Excellent man,' said the Archdeacon. 'Most people
talk such nonsense on these occasions.'

'He's a very fair scholar,' said Canon Stuart. 'They say
he'll probably get the diocese when the old man goes;
does most of the work already. A very sound man, no
modernist nonsense.'

'Four hundred yards, Anthony Stuart.'

'Congratulations,' said the Archdeacon to Tony's
father. 'That man Knight is an arrant Modernist.'

'Can't do the boys much harm at their age,' said
Canon Stuart.

'The bishop's a divine man,' said Charlotte Wimbush.
'But, my dear, such a trying shade of purple! He must
find it very difficult to wear.'

CHAPTER SIXTEEN

Most of the parents had gone; one or two still stood about in front of the house in last talk with their boys, and most of the staff hovered in attendance.

Mary Langton and Kit were talking to the bishop.

'Lucky fellow, to be going back to Italy!' said the bishop. 'If I were only a poet and not a bishop! I should like to live somewhere on the gulf of Spezia.'

'You might retire there one day,' said Mary.

'Yes; it might be rather jolly to be a chaplain to the English visitors,' said the bishop. 'A life of teashops and Tauchnitz novels, very restful. And none of those "opportunities for work with young people" that clergymen are always advertising for. I can't think why they like them so much; I hate them.'

'You might find my husband and me already settled there,' said Mary.

'Oh, you mustn't leave here for ages,' said the bishop.

'May we have a bathe, sir?' said Michael Park, approaching Dudley, who looked very sulky.

'Well, it wouldn't be a bad end to the day, would it?' said Dudley. 'You really ought to ask Mr Henderson, but he's busy talking to his lordship.' Dudley's voice became very sarcastic. 'But cut along, and I'll tell him.'

'But how can we get in, sir?' said Michael.

'Well, now I have something to confess,' said Dudley. 'I've done something a bit offside. I had a bathe before lunch, and I didn't lock the place up. I thought I might be showing it to parents, you know, or even to his lordship—though I should hardly expect him to be interested.'

'Thank you, sir,' said Michael.

'Only sixth form boys, mind,' said Dudley. 'You can tell the other fellows.'

He hung about on the fringe of the group that was dominated by the bishop in his purple cassock.

'People are fond of saying that "England's good enough for them",' said the bishop. 'And on a day like today, and in a garden like yours, Mrs Langton, one can just see what they mean. But, alas, such times and places are the exception.'

'There's no sea but the Mediterranean,' said Kit.

'I beg your pardon, my Lord; I'm sorry to butt in, Christopher,' said Dudley. 'But I ought to tell you that (at his request) I let young Park and a few others go to the swimming-bath.'

'You unlocked it?' asked Kit sharply.

'It's been unlocked all day, in case anyone wanted to look at it. Didn't you know?'

'I knew nothing of this,' said Kit. 'I must go there, this minute.' And he took a hasty leave of the bishop.

He went through the house, and at the back he found Nan Hackett standing. Her hand gripped, and in no tender fashion, Michael Park by the bare shoulder. He was naked, but for his bathing slip, and barefoot; he was still wet from the bath, out of breath from running and in tears.

'How dare you come up to the house in this state, Michael?' said Nan. 'There are visitors still here; what would they think?'

'I must see Mr Henderson at once,' said the boy.

'"Must" isn't a word to use to ladies,' said Nan. 'You'll see no one till you're fit to be seen.'

'Excuse me, Miss Hackett,' said Kit, with icy politeness. 'I think this may be important.'

Michael told his story. 'We were swimming about, Ralph and I. Guy and Tony were there too, and one or two others. Then we heard screams. George and Ronald had got hold of Harry; this time they only half undressed him, and George pushed him in.'

'I'll come at once,' said Kit. 'Mr Knight only told me this minute that some of you were bathing. He will be very much horrified at what has happened.'

'Will he?' asked Michael scornfully. But he made a sign that there was more to tell.

George and Ronald had, no doubt, meant to undress Harry (whom they had waylaid, and frog-marched to the swimming-pool) the moment they saw that no master was in attendance. But Harry had put up a fierce resistance, and had bitten hard into George's thumb. With an angry yell of pain, George let him go, and then barged him violently into the pool, at the deep end.

'You'll get into trouble for that,' said Ronald delightedly. It was a serious offence at Hazelcroft to damage one's own or another boy's clothes.

They waited for Harry to come out.

'Everyone can swim when he has to,' said George, but Harry showed no sign of possessing this ability.

'I must get him out,' said Michael. 'Good chance to practise life-saving!'

Harry was pulled to the side, and then, by the combined efforts of several boys, hauled on to the grass. He was unconscious.

'I don't like it,' said Guy.

'I bet he's shamming,' said Ronald. 'Tickle his nose with grass.'

'I don't hear him breathing,' said Tony, who had undone his shirt.

'I can't find his pulse,' said Guy.

'How can he breathe, if you all crowd round him like that?' said Ralph.

'I shall fetch Kit; he ought to be here,' said Michael.

'Ass! Then he'll find out everything that's happened,' said someone. 'We'll all get into a horrible row, not only George. Let's do some artificial respiration. We'll bring him round before Henderson comes, and make him say he fell in.'

They worked at Harry's arms a bit.

'He couldn't drown in a minute like that?' said Tony, in a shocked voice.

'Other things could happen,' said Ralph. 'He might have knocked his head against the side, or his heart may have failed. I'm afraid he's dead.'

Tony, almost automatically, made the sign of the cross; then he burst out crying, Guy put an arm round him, and with the other hand held his head against his shoulder.

'I can't stand it; I'm going to the house for someone,' said Michael.

'Not just as you are?' said Ronald in a shocked voice.

'Just as I am,' said Michael, and sped away.

'Miss Hackett, I shall go there at once with Michael,' said Kit. 'Will you please tell Matron and my uncle? They ought to come at once.'

'The headmaster will be saying goodbye to people,' said Nan. 'And Matron will be having to put the younger boys to bed.'

'You and Mr Knight can do all that,' said Kit with impatience. 'This is serious.'

'Don't you think Michael is exaggerating?' said Miss Hackett.

'I'm afraid not,' said Kit, laying a gentle hand upon the boy's shoulder, which was still red from Nan's grip. 'I hope and pray things are a bit better than he thinks,

153

though. Otherwise it's the end of the school, and so it ought to be!'

Kit arrived at the bath to find a shivering and weeping group of boys. Two of them were working, now without hope, on Harry's arms. He made a quick inspection, and was in no way reassured.

'Get dressed quickly, all of you,' he said. 'I'll stay with Harry. Matron will come and bring him some brandy. And the headmaster is coming.'

He sent the boys up to the school; they were now excited, and in those tearing high spirits that succeed grief and shock in the young. They hailed the headmaster and Matron as they passed them. A little later they met Peggy, burdened with blankets.

'Peggy, how's Peggy?' called someone.

'She's preggy!' cried Ralph.

They went on their way, not knowing that she had fallen down with her burden. Matron, the headmaster and Kit, returning with the limp body of Harry, found her in convulsions. That night it was clear that there would be no issue of her connection with the former knife and boot man.

The staff supper was late that night. Matron was summoned from hers (brought up to her on a tray) by Michael Park from the Grey Room; Tony was crying uncontrollably.

'My dear, I'll bring Guy in from the Mauve Room, and put him in poor Harry's bed for tonight,' she said. 'They're great friends, and Tony will like to have him there.'

'Thank you, Matron,' said Michael. 'I shall like that too.'

'You're sleeping in a dead man's bed,' said Ronald, when Guy came in. 'You're a brave chap; I hope he won't haunt you.'

'You *are* a nasty little beast,' said Guy. 'I've nothing against dead people; my own brother is dead. And poor Harry had nothing against *me*.'

Nan, meanwhile, had got hold of Dudley, and was pouring out her scruples; had she kept Michael waiting a minute when he brought the news? If she had run straight to the swimming-bath with him, could she have been in time to do something? Would she be haunted by this all her life?

'Ah, no, Nan,' said Dudley. 'You will come, in the end, to see infinite mercy at work, here as everywhere— even in this ending of a young life that might not have developed very happily.'

'But could I have been in time?'

'Ah, no, Nan; he wasn't drowned,' said Dudley. 'You couldn't have made his heart start to beat again.'

'We made life such a burden to him,' said Nan, with a choking voice. 'And he had such a short time to live.'

'If we'd managed to make more of a man of him, he might be alive now—if it was God's will.'

'Oh, anything might happen if it was God's will,' said Nan with impatience.

'Nan, I don't think you know what you're saying,' said Dudley.

'I'm sorry; I daresay I don't,' said Nan.

'You must try to control yourself,' said Dudley. 'We shall have to mind our step these days. If we do, I think some good may come even out of this terrible tragedy. But I must have a word with Mrs Langton.'

Mary Langton was at her bureau, in her upstairs drawing-room, trying to write a letter to Harry's mother.

'Mrs Langton,' I would like to talk to you a moment about a delicate matter,' said Dudley. 'I'm told that girl, Peggy, is in a certain condition.'

'We're all in one condition or another,' said Mary.

'She certainly is, but I don't think she'll be in it for long; she's having a miscarriage.'

'And I wasn't told!' said Dudley.

'Oh, poor girl, she asked to stay till the end of the term,' said Mary. 'She didn't want you to know; I daresay she was afraid you would cast the first stone.'

'Ah, no, poor girl!' said Dudley. 'I'm sure she was more sinned against than sinning. But we have to think of the boys; such an example for them!'

'Being boys, they cannot follow her example,' said Mary. 'I did not think they would know anything about it, and I hope they don't.'

'I'm told one of the boys said something to her, and caused this collapse,' said Dudley. 'We must get to the bottom of this.'

Mary threw down her pen, and stood up. 'We must do nothing of the kind, Mr Knight,' she said. 'The boys have been tried enough; I forbid you to worry them about this.'

'"Forbid" is a very strong word, Mrs Langton, from you to me,' said Dudley.

'I'm afraid I must use strong words,' said Mary. 'I respect your position in the school; but I am the first woman here, and the boys' mothers will put the responsibility for their children on me.'

He cast his eyes down.

'Yes, you needn't envy me for that!' said Mary. 'Here am I, in the most bitter grief and shame, trying to write to the mother of that poor child who has been done to death.'

'Not very much of a mother to him, I believe,' said Dudley.

'I thought you were a Christian,' said Mary. 'Doesn't it occur to you that the poor woman will be suffering all the more, because she must feel that she could have done more for him? I feel that myself; I don't quite know what more I could have done, but I ought to have known it, and done it.'

'Ah, we must all feel something like that,' said Dudley with a sigh.

'I think you must feel a bit more than that,' said Mary. 'It was you who left the bath unlocked, and it was that horrible thug whom you encouraged who killed the poor boy.'

'We must be careful of our words, Mrs Langton,' said Dudley. 'We don't want to ruin the school; your husband won't want to have to sell his share in it for a song.'

Mary looked at him in amazement.

'Let's forget anything that has been said between us that had better not have been said,' he continued.

'We will leave it like that for the moment,' said Mary. 'And you will leave Peggy and her story alone.'

'Yes,' said Dudley. 'The domestic staff is your province, Mrs Langton. And we shall have other things to think of these days.'

Nan Hackett and Anita Rigby, unusually united, went up to the latter's room after supper; neither liked being alone.

The headmaster sat in his study, drumming on the desk with his fingers; presently Dudley came in to see him.

Dick Langton went upstairs to join his wife in the drawing-room.

'Where's Kit?' he asked.

'In the garden,' said Mary. 'I expect he's crying; and at his age one wouldn't want anyone to see. He was very near it at supper.'

'We'll have a drink when he comes in,' said Langton. 'We need it.'

Soon Kit's step was heard.

'I'm glad you've come up, Christopher darling,' said Mary with especial warmth. 'Sit here.' She chose a chair where the light did not fall upon him, and avoided looking him in the eyes, for she rightly imagined his to be red.

'Dudley has pointed a pistol to our heads,' said Dick Langton. 'I'm to retire, to save the school; you're to take the blame for not knowing that the bath was open.'

'My God!' said Kit. 'That Girling creature ought to be strung up; Dudley ought to be unfrocked, and he and Nan sent to hard labour for life as accessories before the fact.'

'I defend Nan,' said Mary. 'I never thought I should. She's really cut up.'

'They don't hang boys of George's age, Kit,' said his uncle.

'More's the pity!' said Kit fiercely. 'But they can be sent to reformatories.'

'I shouldn't care,' said Dick. 'But he didn't mean to throw poor Harry in. Knight says he was acting in self-defence, as the poor boy was biting his thumb.'

'Self-defence!' said Kit. 'Harry was being tortured; I wish he'd bitten George's disgusting nose off!'

'You're right,' said Mary. 'But it wouldn't be any good unfrocking Dudley; he hardly is very frocked, if you see what I mean.'

'Have some brandy, Kit, you need it,' said Dick Langton.

'Dudley's plan is of a stark simplicity,' said Mary. 'You take the rap—if there is any rap—as it won't hurt your future. Your uncle and I retire, as a sop to any parents who think something may have gone wrong with the school; and Dudley goes on—as I think he would say—from strength to strength.'

'Good God!' said Kit. 'I'm not sure that I'm going to

play his game. Suppose we go out to make all the stink possible!'

'You won't bring Harry back to life,' said Mary, sadly.

'Poor little beast!' said Kit. 'Would one if one could? He mightn't thank one. But there is such a thing as abstract justice.'

'Rather an inconvenient thing,' said Mary. 'You're very young, dearest boy.'

'I shall not ask you to act against your conscience,' said his uncle. 'I have no right. But if you make a stink, you will ruin your aunt and me, as well as Knight. The school would go to pot. If Knight takes on, he has to pay us—so and so much down, and a share in the profits for a number of years.'

'So he has us in a cleft stick?' said Kit. 'All right, Dudley shall flourish like the green bay tree, though the thought of it makes me sick.'

'You'd better start looking out for somewhere for us to live, when you get back to Italy,' said Mary. 'One day we will talk about it all there, and perhaps with that sweet bishop.'

'I don't suppose there's any good golf to be had there,' said Dick. 'But I'll soon be past it.'

'You'll be a don at Cambridge,' said Mary. 'But you must come to us often in vacations. We can't live without you, Christopher dear, after all we've been through together. We'll have a charming garden.'

'I ask nothing better,' said Christopher. 'But I'll miss the beech tree.'

'Knight will have it down,' said his uncle.

CHAPTER SEVENTEEN

The inquest was held in the Church Hall, and the coroner was the local doctor, who was anxious to make as little trouble for anyone as he needed. Lady Best-Pennant was there, a grim black figure; she was supported by a solicitor, who sometimes asked awkward questions. Death was found to be due to natural causes; Harry had not been drowned. The jury added a rider, that boys should not be left unattended in a swimming-bath.

Surprisingly, Lady Best-Pennant came up to Kit, and offered him a hand. 'You were good to the poor boy,' she said.

Dick Langton went gloomily back to the school and sat in his study, drafting and redrafting the letter that was to be printed for circulation among the parents. It was to announce his impending retirement, and the continuation of the school under the capable direction of his present partner, the Reverend Dudley Knight.

'Shall we announce your forthcoming marriage at the same time, Mr Knight?' Mary had asked. 'Parents like there to be a woman at the head of things.'

'That would be rather premature,' said Dudley. 'No woman has yet done me the honour to promise to become my wife.'

'Well, you could go and ask one of them before we send the letter to the printers.'

'You will have your joke, Mrs Langton,' said Dudley. 'But I happen to take a serious view of marriage. And till the right man meets the right maid...'

'No wedding bells, then?' said Mary. 'No "mirth in funeral and dirge in marriage"?'

'My mother will join forces with me,' said Dudley.

'You may find that other staff changes are necessary,' said Mary. 'You may have to start next term with an entirely new staff.'

'Mrs Langton, I shall not flinch from it,' said Dudley.

In the Grey Room a far more searching inquest was held.

'Who's to be judge?' asked Hugh.

'There's only a coroner, you ass,' said Michael. 'Tony will do. Bags I appearing for Harry's family! Ralph, you've got to appear for the creature Girling's family.'

'What a disgusting idea!' said Ralph.

'You've got to do your best; no one must be able to say that we condemned him without a fair trial,' said Michael, moving the scene from a coroner's court to a court of assize.

'You seem to have condemned me in advance,' said George.

'Not at all,' said Ralph. 'You shall have every chance. But it's pretty obvious, isn't it?'

'Hugh, you're the clerk,' said Michael. 'You've got to ask the prisoner at the bar how he wishes to be tried.'

'Prisoner at the bar, how do you wish to be tried?'

'I don't want to be tried at all,' said George. 'I think this is a rotten game. I shall tell the Dud.'

'You have to say: "By God and my country",' said Michael.

'I don't think we ought to bring God in,' said Tony.

'I don't agree; it's serious enough,' said Michael. 'Prisoner at the bar, you'd better choose to be tried by God and your country, or we might be forced to try you by ordeal.'

'By God and my country,' said George, sulkily.

'Who's his country?' asked Tony. 'Does that mean us?'

'I hadn't thought of that,' said Michael. 'We must have a jury. I know. Hugh shall keep notes, and we'll send them to the Mauve Room.'

'They'll laugh at this kid's game,' said George.

'Guy won't,' said Michael.

'What about Ronald?' said Tony.

'What about him?' said Michael. 'Beg Lordship's pardon,' and he gave a rapid bow.

'I mean, are we going to try him too as a—what d'you call it?'

'Accomplice before the fact, me Lud,' said Michael. 'I think you might ask him Tony—I mean, me Lud—if he'll turn King's Evidence. If he'll give evidence against George—I mean the accused—we might let him off being tried. We really rather need a witness.'

'Will you turn King's Evidence?' asked Tony.

'Oh, yes,' said Ronald. 'I was only ragging with poor Harry. I never thought George was going to do what he did.'

'Well, I kick off,' said Michael. 'I'm the counsel for the prosecution, Sir Michael Park, K.C., and you have to call me "the learned counsel". I'm going to tell you what happened. About seven o'clock on the evening of Sports Day, the accused, George Alfred Girling came in at the door to the swimming bath. He and my witness, Master Ronald Wedderburn Gibson, pushed or pulled in with them the deceased Henry Edward Staples. They proceeded to try to undress the deceased, who resisted them; in fact he bit hard into the prisoner's disgusting thumb, and I don't know how it didn't make him sick. It was evidently their intention to throw him into the bath. The prisoner let go, and began blubbing with pain; at the same time he barged poor Harry—the deceased—into the bath, which directly caused his death from shock. That is my case, my Lord; and I ask for the prisoner Girling to be found guilty of wilful murder, and to be hanged by the neck.'

'I don't quite understand, Sir Michael,' said Tony. 'We don't know that the prisoner meant poor Harry to die of shock; I don't believe he did.'

'With great respect, me Lud,' said Michael. 'Your Lordship is supposed to instruct us about the law; but as you don't know a thing about it, I'd better tell you. If you kill somebody while you're committing a crime —and it was a horrid crime to bully poor Harry—then you're guilty of murder, even if you didn't want them to die. We'll have to pretend you said all that, not me. Hugh, put it down as Lord Chief Justice Stuart's opinion.'

'I haven't any more paper,' said Hugh.

'Then you must say: "the court is adjourned",' said Michael.

'The court is adjourned,' said Tony. 'Any way it's nearly silence time.'

The trial was resumed in the evening.

'Call Master Ronald Wedderburn Gibson,' said Hugh.

Ronald was sworn upon the Bible.

'Did you help the accused, George Alfred Girling, to drag the deceased Henry Edward Staples in at the door of the swimming-bath?' asked Michael.

'Yes,' said Ronald. 'But I never meant...'

'You started undressing him?'

'We were only ragging.'

'Then you let go; why?'

'He was biting George's thumb,' said Ronald.

'The deceased was biting the prisoner's thumb,' said Michael. 'And I daresay you did not want him to hurt you?'

'No,' said Ronald. 'Then George let go of his hand, and barged him into the bath.'

'Very well,' said Michael, going back to the business of brushing his teeth. 'Your witness, Sir Ralph.'

'How did you get Harry in there?' said Ralph.

'He was quite near, looking at the rabbit hutches,' said Ronald. 'He was fond of rabbits.'

'He didn't come with you willingly?'

'Is it likely?' said Ronald.

'Well, I can't get much out of him,' said Ralph. 'Do I make my speech now? Well, me Lud, and gentlemen of the Jury—though you can't hear me—I'm not quite convinced that the case against the accused has been made out. The witness against him is the creature Ronald Wedderburn Gibson; he may have sworn to tell the truth, but we know that he can't, even if he wants to. And he's been practically forced to turn King's Evidence, anyhow. And though I think it most wrong and unkind to push poor Harry—the deceased, I mean —into the bath, you know Mr Langton did it once. I don't think Mr Langton would commit a crime; he would know better. I ask for a verdict of manslaughter.'

Tony, assisted by a hastily scribbled note from Michael, summed up.

'The learned counsel for the defence should not say that the witness Ronald Wedderburn Gibson was forced to give evidence; I'm in charge of this court, and I could not allow anything so improper. As the facts are pretty well admitted by everyone, even by the prisoner himself (I don't know why Sir Ralph didn't call on him to give evidence), we can believe them, even if the witness Gibson tells them to us. It is true that the head-master did on one occasion push the deceased into the bath, but he was wearing the belt, so he knew quite well he couldn't drown. If the gentlemen of the jury want any help from me in reaching their verdict, I'll try to worm a bit more medical evidence out of Kit Henderson.'

An obliging maid, coming in with a vast can of hot water, promised to convey the papers to the Mauve Room. Next morning she told them that the Mauve Room sent congratulations to them all, particularly to Ralph, on his brilliant defence.

'Heavens, have I got the horrid creature off?' said Ralph.

'I hope they're congratulating my learned friend on making the best of a bad job,' said Michael. 'That point about the headmaster was very clever.'

A little later the same obliging maid came back, smirking, and handed a note to Tony: 'Guilty as Hell.'

After confabulation with Michael, Tony coiled up a black tie, put it on his head, and said: 'Prisoner at the bar, after a fair trial you have been convicted of the foul crime of murder, in spite of a most brilliant defence by your learned counsel. I therefore have much pleasure in sentencing you to be hanged by the neck until you are dead. As, unfortunately, I am unable to have this just sentence carried out, I sentence you to Coventry for life. None of us will speak to you again (unless we're obliged to say a word or two in the presence of the staff). You are dead to us. This is the last word that will be addressed to you by anyone in this room.'

'What do we do if we have to tell him to shut up, or something?' asked Hugh.

'We refer to him in the third person,' said Michael. 'We say: "the low criminal" or "the swine Girling had better shut up".'

'It's almost treating him like Royalty, to use the third person, I mean,' said Ralph. 'But what else can one do?'

'We have to remember that the criminal Girling is in Coventry, where bicycles come from,' said Michael that night. 'He's not here. We may say exactly what we like about him.'

'And about his father and mother, and everything that is his,' said Ralph.

'I say!' said Tony.

'Ralph is quite right,' said Michael. 'There are no limits.'

'He won't be able to stay on at Hazelcroft,' said Ralph. 'It's our business to make that impossible, even if they consent to keep him.'

'They'd hardly want to keep a murderer,' said Hugh.

'Dick wouldn't make any sacrifices for him,' said Michael. 'I believe he takes him at a reduced rate already.'

'The Brigadier worked that,' said Ronald. 'He said he was poor.'

'Fancy reducing the fees for such a stupid boy!' said Ralph. 'If he scrapes into a public school, it's the most he'll do.'

'No good school would take him now,' said Michael. 'They've all got pretty well booked up. No need to take a boy of bad character.'

'He won't get into the Army now,' said Ronald.

'Not as an officer, of course,' said Michael. 'But I've no doubt he could get in without a commission—they'll take any trash.'

'He could hardly do that,' said Tony. 'After all, he's a gentleman.'

'I suppose his father's a gentleman,' admitted Ralph. 'But his mother's a very common little person; my mater said so.'

George gave a howl of rage.

'It's pretty steep to talk like that about a chap's mater in front of him,' said Tony.

'The low criminal Girling is in Coventry, let me

166

remind you,' said Michael. 'We must talk as if he wasn't here.'

'I wonder how his father came to marry her?' said Hugh. 'I wonder how they met?'

'Oh, I expect she was some low camp follower sort of person,' said Michael.

There was another howl of rage. George may not have greatly loved his mother, but his own pride had been dragged in the dust.

'Why *marry* her?' said Ralph. 'Really I think it was very honourable of the Brigadier—pompous bore though he is. I suppose George was on the way, and he thought he ought to make an honest woman of her.'

'More than the knife and boot man did for poor Peggy,' said Michael.

'But what do you mean?' said Tony. 'Surely it's only the lower classes that are born that way? Our sort of people have to be married first.'

'Tony, you're sweet,' said Ralph. 'I quite understand why everyone is in love with you, though you're not my type. Poor Harry was crazy about you.'

Tony burst into tears.

'Tony, I'm sorry; I didn't want to make you cry,' said Ralph.

'You didn't choose a very good way not to,' said Michael.

'I was fond of him,' said Tony. 'I liked him better than anyone, except Guy.'

'Then we'll avenge him,' said Michael bracingly.

'I'll be all right,' said George. 'Dick is retiring, and the Dud will take over the school, next term. You hadn't thought of that, had you?'

'Perhaps we'd better be careful,' said Ronald.

'You heard the disgusting remark of the swine Girling,' said Michael. 'I happen to know as much as he does. But if Deadly Nightshade wants to make a success of this school, he won't want to lose you, Ralph, or you, Tony, or me. We could all easily get in elsewhere; though I think it would be a mistake at this stage in our education. Deadly Nightshade is an efficient schoolmaster. But we've all got family connections, and nothing against us—if he has to choose between us and the swine Girling. . . .'

'Of course he must choose us,' said Ralph.

'He will probably have to choose,' said Michael.

'Lord, I'm sorry for Kit,' said Ralph.

'Was he very fond of Harry?' said Tony, tearfully.

'I think he liked you and me and Michael as much, if not better,' said Ralph. 'As we are, I mean. He was interested in what Harry was going to be; and the swine Girling has knocked all that on the head.'

'Literally,' said Michael.

'Kit has been crying a lot lately,' said Ralph. 'I've seen his eyes.'

'Crying at his age!' said Ronald, contemptuously.

'My father cries, when people in the village die,' said Tony. 'I like Kit; I wish he was staying.'

'The school won't be much of a place, unless they get good new staff,' said Michael. 'There's not much to stay for.'

'But we mustn't give it up to the swine Girling,' said Tony.

'And it will be faintly interesting to see whether Nan or Anita hooks Deadly Nightshade,' said Ralph.

CHAPTER EIGHTEEN

'It would be nice to have a little service to com-
memorate poor Harry Staples, don't you think?' said
Dudley. 'And it would show the boys that it isn't to be
an awkward subject.'

'Nice, indeed, Mr Knight!' said Mary. 'What a gift
you have for choosing the right word! And otherwise
they might think we did but greenly in hugger-mugger
so to cremate him.'

'Something quite simple,' said Dudley. 'And cheery,
you know. Not dwelling too much on death, but giving
thanks for his life.'

'I see no grounds for cheerfulness or thankfulness,'
said Mary. 'Though perhaps it's as well for him that life
is over. No address, please, Mr Knight; that I must insist
on.'

Dudley pouted, for it was in the address that he had
hoped to use all his powers.

'You can work some of it into the prayers,' said Mary,
seeing his disappointment. 'I've no doubt the Almighty
knows all you can tell Him, but I suppose at His age He
is past being embarrassed.'

'And the hymns?' said Dudley, deliberately ignoring
her sally.

'They will be my choice,' said Mary.

This, of course, promised a discordant element in the
cheerful, manly little form of prayer that Dudley had
devised.

Dick, however, did not wish to take part, and Dudley

could show independence of convention by choosing a lesson from the *Pilgrim's Progress,* instead of the Bible. It could not have been worse chosen, for it was the passing of Mr Valiant-for-Truth:

'Many accompanied him to the river-side, into which as he went he said, Death, where is thy sting? And as he went down deeper he said, Grave where is thy victory?'

'My God!' murmured Mary. 'Hymn five hundred and thirty-six: *There is a land of pure delight,'* she said aloud. 'I can be cruel too,' she said to Kit.

They sang:

> *But timorous mortals start and shrink*
> *To cross the narrow sea,*
> *And linger shivering on the brink,*
> *And fear to launch away.*

Dudley then addressed a few cheerful and rather impertinent prayers to the Almighty, containing some inaccurate information, and some breezy false sentiment about 'the great adventure that men call Death'.

In sepulchral tones, Mary gave out hymn three hundred and ninety-nine: *When our heads are bow'd with woe.*

A good many handkerchiefs came out, and there was audible sniffing.

'And now,' said Mary, 'I am going to write to poor Harry's mother what a nice little service we had.'

Dudley came up to the drawing-room after luncheon.

'That poor fellow George Girling is having a bad time,' he said. 'The boys seem to pick on him as responsible for this tragedy, and they're making his life a burden.'

'I'm very glad to hear it,' said Mary.

'They're not using physical violence?' asked Dick Langton anxiously.

'No, Headmaster, but his feelings...'

'Has he any feelings?' asked Kit, now joining in his relations' open warfare against Dudley.

'I shan't interfere,' said Dick Langton.

'You know, his father may have to take him away,' said Dudley.

'That will do the school no harm,' said Dick. 'We don't make much profit on him.'

'That's a very cynical remark,' said Dudley, with a nervous laugh.

'Listen, Knight,' said Dick Langton. 'You're not the man to talk about cynicism, after the opportunist way in which you ousted my wife and me; I can talk like this, now that we cannot pretend to be friends any more, except in front of the boys.'

'Oh, Headmaster, you were both and will ever be the best of friends in my thoughts,' said Dudley.

' "The best of friends must part, must part",' sang Mary. 'And what a mercy that is!'

'My wife and I are leaving for the good of the school —that is, for its financial good,' said Dick Langton. 'In every other way I think it will be the worse for our going. If you don't jettison George Girling—who is no loss—you may lose Michael Park, Ralph Wimbush and Tony Stuart. Those boys are assets: Michael will get an Eton or Winchester scholarship, Ralph has family connections, and Tony will win your cricket matches for you. You can't afford to lose those boys, and I can't afford to let you risk it.'

'I must yield to pressure,' said Dudley. 'But you won't mind if I speak to those fellows, Headmaster, and appeal to what is best in them?'

Dick thought for a moment, 'I make three conditions,' he said. 'You must make no threat of any sort to these

171

boys—they are to feel that the school is proud of them. Next, anything you do must be done off your own bat; you mustn't mention my wife or me. And lastly, you must expect no help from me, if your talk with them doesn't go off as you would like it.'

'You are hard, Headmaster, but I accept,' said Dudley. 'You and Christopher won't put them up to resist me?'

'My uncle and I are not devious,' said Kit.

Dudley began his campaign at school tea. It was indoors, as it was a dark day; and the Langtons were not present.

'No one is speaking to Girling,' he observed. 'Give him a share in the conversation.'

'*Il fait beau temps, il tombe d'eau, il va pleuvoir,*' said Ralph.

'*Que fait Monsieur le Curé?*' said Michael, catching on.

'*Où est la plume de ma tante?*' asked Tony, after reflection.

George's nose looked more and more enflamed.

'Stop it!' said Dudley. 'What's all this nonsense?'

'Don't you like us making French conversation, sir?' asked Ralph, in an injured tone. 'At some schools it's the rule at meals.'

'It isn't at Hazelcroft,' said Dudley. 'English is good enough for us.'

'What is Monsieur le Curé doing?' asked Ralph.

'Have you the pen of the gardener's wife?' asked Michael.

'It is nine o'clock in the morning,' said Tony.

'What's all this gibberish?' blustered Dudley.

'You told us to speak, sir,' said Michael. 'We are speaking.'

'You're not speaking naturally.'

'It doesn't come naturally to us to speak to the person whom you mentioned, sir,' said Michael. 'We should not speak to him if we were alone.'

'I shall have something to say about this another time,' said Dudley grimly.

He called the three boys to his study next day.

'I want to talk about this nonsense of yours with Girling,' he said impatiently. 'It's having a bad effect on the school.'

'He has only to leave the school,' said Ralph.

'We've sent him permanently to Coventry,' said Michael.

'What a childish game!' said Dudley. 'Haven't you grown out of such things?'

'My grandfather and grandmother lived twenty-five years together, without speaking a word to each other in private,' said Ralph. 'They were both over fifty when this began.'

'We don't care to speak to a killer,' said Michael.

'Take care, take care,' said Dudley. 'You know, if you say things like that his father may bring an action for libel?'

'Slander,' corrected Michael. 'I don't think he'll care to advertise his son's part in Harry's death.'

'Brigadier Girling is very angry and indignant at the way his son is being treated.'

'Well, what of it?' asked Michael, with scorn.

'That doesn't impress you?' said Dudley. 'A high-ranking officer four times your age...'

'A retired military man of no importance,' said Michael. 'We are far more important in this school than he is.'

'Are you,' said Dudley sarcastically. 'Three little boys!'

'Yes, we're the bright hopes of the future,' said Ralph. 'If we wanted to leave, any school would lap us up: the

killer Girling can only get into some school for backward boys—if they'll take him after this.'

'Oh, you're too clever to live!' said Dudley with
disgust. 'But, if you're gentlemen, you'll respect a distinguished officer who has served his country well, and
risked his life for you. . . .'

'I don't think so,' said Tony. 'He was in India all
through the war.'

'I've never heard that he'd done anything much,' said
Ralph.

'Some people aren't always talking about what they've
done,' said Dudley.

'That family is,' said Michael. 'And any way it isn't
the Brigadier whom we've sent to Coventry, but his
nasty son.'

'And there's another thing,' said Dudley. 'I hear you
have dared to speak against his parents, and in front of
him.'

'Oh, he's sneaked, has he?' said Michael.

'I thought he would,' said Tony.

'Do you expect him to listen to you abusing his
father?' said Dudley. 'And his mother too—the most
sacred thing a boy has in the world?'

'Why more sacred than a grandmother?' asked Ralph.
'Or a great-uncle, or a first cousin once removed?'

'Pah!' said Dudley. 'I'm tired of the lot of you.'

'You started this conversation, sir,' said Michael.

'We weren't talking in front of the low criminal
Girling, but behind his back,' said Ralph. 'He's in
Coventry.'

'A quibble that is unworthy of you, Wimbush,'
said Dudley. 'And worse is to come; you have spoken
rudely of a lady. That is a thing no gentleman should
do.'

'That I am sure I haven't,' said Ralph. 'My mother
wouldn't like it at all.'

174

'I'm told you have spoken most rudely about Mrs Girling.'

'Oh, her!' said Michael.

'She's not a lady,' said Ralph. 'My mother told me she was a very common little person.'

'With all respect to your good mother, Wimbush, we don't talk about that sort of thing here.'

'Oh, why not, sir? Isn't it quite nice?' asked Ralph eagerly.

'D'you mean "her moral standard is not our own"?' said Michael. 'As you said about Rahab, when we asked you what a harlot was?'

'You can't possibly understand what you're saying,' said Dudley. 'That must be your excuse.'

He cleared his throat, and started again: 'Instead of just appealing to your better nature, and such sense as you have, I could order you to stop this futile business of Coventry.'

'I'm afraid we should have to disobey you, sir,' said Michael. 'We've sworn on our sacred oath.'

'Oh, you have, have you?' said Dudley. 'Well, I'm your scout-master; what about your scout's promise to obey me? Can there be a more sacred oath?'

'Oh, that!' said Ralph, in contempt.

'Surely it only means anything when we're playing at Boy Scouts?' said Michael.

'Playing at Boy Scouts!' repeated Dudley, in something between sorrow and anger. 'You're scouts at every minute of the day and night.'

'Well we were forced into that absurdity,' said Ralph. 'We'll resign.'

'You can't,' said Dudley. 'Once a scout, always a scout.'

'But, sir, it can't be like that,' said Michael. 'What about all the boys who have left school? They can't go on obeying you, even if they want to.'

'Well, perhaps the scout promise does lapse,' admitted Dudley.

'And you can be degraded from the scouts,' said Michael. 'I'm sure I've read about that being done. Why not degrade us?'

'Oh, don't let's speak of anything so disagreeable!' said Dudley. 'You wouldn't like anything of the sort to happen to you.'

'We should love it!' said Michael.

'Fix a day in advance, please sir!' said Ralph. 'Then my mother can come down, and we'll make a party of it. She'll be delighted; she hates those nigger-brown shirts we have to wear with our scout-clothes here, and those sea-green scarves.'

'If that is all it is to you!' said Dudley sorrowfully.

'It's nothing to us!' said the boys in chorus.

'He won't dare do it,' said Tony, when Dudley had left them.

'Of course not, but what sport if he did!' said Michael. 'My pater would ask a question about it in the House.'

'It would be fun to be martyrs, without giving up anything we like,' said Ralph.

'To get off those boring old parades, and just go for a short walk with Matron,' said Michael. 'And then come back and read a book!'

'Heavenly!' sighed Ralph.

'But I'm afraid my pater wouldn't like it,' said Michael. 'He's rather conventional.'

'I've come to believe that, in the boy's own interest, we ought to advise Brigadier Girling to find another school for his son,' said Dudley heavily.

'Oh, you are there at last?' said Langton. 'That was my opinion from the first.'

'There's this unaccountable prejudice against him among the boys,' said Dudley.

'I can easily account for it; I share it,' said Mary.

'I have a distinct recollection of your saying that if boys take it into their own hands to deal with each other, they generally have a reason,' said Kit. 'I didn't agree with you at the time, and I still think the bully ought to be put down. But when Michael and Ralph and Tony get together in this way, I feel proud of them —they're beginning to behave like good citizens of the future.'

'So they haven't given way? Dear, brave boys!' said Mary. 'I should like to go and kiss them, if I didn't know they'd hate it.'

'George Girling will be no loss,' said Kit.

'Christopher, I know you're very clever and all that,' said Dudley. 'But perhaps you don't yet fully know how to value simple worth and loyalty. You will, one day, dear boy; I know you're really sound at heart.'

'Too kind!' said Kit.

'And what's to become of the poor lad?' asked Dudley.

'I think I can get him in at Bengers Towers,' said Dick Langton.

'That's not much of a place for him,' said Dudley. 'A crank staff, and a lot of wrecks—and they say some of them aren't quite—'

'Quite of one's own class, you mean?' said Dick Langton, who scorned a euphemism. 'No, they'll take anyone; even Niggers and Sheenies.'

Dudley shuddered.

'They're trying to build themselves up again,' said Dudley. 'They had a bit of trouble last year, when one of the partners suddenly had to go abroad. Lost some boys then.'

'You mean?' said Dudley.

'Oh, the usual thing,' said Dick Langton, in a matter-of-fact way. 'They're sure to have vacancies, and it's a pretty cheap school—suit the Brigadier.'

'You mean, you are sending this boy into a den of immorality?' said Dudley.

'Oh, I expect it's all been cleaned up by now,' said Dick.

'George ought to be safe,' said Mary. 'He's such a very plain boy. That nose!'

Dudley blushed, and was silent.

Kit, left alone with Dick, said: 'As a family, we've come out pretty well; we've shocked and annihilated him.'

'I knew I should make him wince,' said Dick. 'He pays lip service to the equality of mankind: "scouts of every colour", don't you know? But of course he doesn't really believe in it any more than the rest of us.'

'And Aunt Mary was magnificent.'

Dick Langton chuckled.

'I feel sorry for Bengers Towers,' said Kit. 'But buggers can't be choosers—if you'll forgive my language.'

'Ha, ha!' said his uncle. 'Mary will enjoy that.'

'Oh, I couldn't tell her,' said Kit.

'Never mind, I can,' said Dick.

CHAPTER NINETEEN

'Anita Rigby and Nan have offered their resignations,' said Mary. 'They say they wouldn't like to stay on at Hazelcroft without your uncle and me.'

'That's very touching,' said Kit. 'But I suppose they have got wind of old Mrs Knight's coming. They've given up hope of Dudley.'

'More than that,' said Mary. 'Nan seems to have conceived a positive horror of him. I think she blames him for poor Harry's death.'

'He certainly cashed in on it pretty quickly,' said Kit. 'There was something rather indecent about his opportunism.'

'Oh, he had a plan ready to oust us, as soon as any scandal occurred in the school,' said Mary. 'The minute this tragedy happened, he just put his little plan into operation; and he'd groomed you as a scape-goat.'

'We can't blame him directly for what has happened,' said Kit. 'But I wonder if Uncle Dick need have let him profit by it.'

'My dear, your uncle was very much more cut up about this than you realize,' said Mary. 'He didn't really want to go on. If he had gone on, it would have meant a perpetual struggle with Dudley—Dudley intriguing with the staff or whispering with parents. He couldn't stand it.'

'It was really Uncle Dick who spoiled Nan's and Anita's chances, then?' said Kit. 'Dudley would have had to go on courting them, if he hadn't got his own way. He might have become engaged to both of them!'

'Not to Nan,' said Mary. 'I don't think he could ever have won her back again.'

'And now those two girls are tremendous chums,' said Kit. 'It's all "Nan dear!" and "Anita darling!"'

'They're trying to get posts at the same school,' said Mary. 'Christopher, dear, do you think these violent friendships between women are quite wholesome?'

'It's all right in this case, I should think,' said Kit. 'They've each lost their ideal—which had come between them until now. They must both be in need of comfort, and where can they turn except to each other?'

'Where, indeed, poor things?' said Mary. 'Dick and I have each other, and you're too young, and Matron is too busy.'

'What I should call an unnatural passion, would be if anyone loved Dudley,' said Kit.

'I shouldn't think anyone did now, except that odious Girling boy,' said Mary. 'And Dudley has let him down.'

'Have any parents threatened to take their boys away?' asked Kit. 'One imagines that happens, if things go wrong.'

'No,' said Mary. 'It doesn't really. It isn't at all easy to find another good school for a boy: boys are put down for here, as often as not, as soon as they're born. A school might make a place for a particularly brilliant boy, like Michael, or a very good cricketer like Tony, and Ralph's Lords might get him in somewhere—but the rank and file could only hope to get in at a Bengers Towers sort of place.'

'So they haven't sent horrid letters?' said Kit.

'No fathers have. I daresay Dick's printed letter did stop any nonsense. I've no doubt that Dudley would have stirred some up.'

'But mothers?'

'They're fools, of course, and rather worse when

they're widowed and uncontrolled,' said Mary. 'Mrs Pilkington wrote to remind me once more that Gussie might come in for an earldom one day, and must be carefully looked after.'

'I don't know what the place will be like without Dick and Mary,' said Michael. 'I feel tempted to go in for a scholarship at one of the schools that have them in the autumn; then I could leave at Christmas.'

'I suppose I could take the entrance exam next term,' said Ralph. 'Mother might send me abroad for two terms if there wasn't a place at Eton before then.'

'And someone might always die there or be sacked,' said Michael.

'And what am I to do?' said Tony indignantly. 'All by myself!'

'No, I expect we'll stay,' said Michael. 'The new staff may not be bad, and Deadly Nightshade will have to eat out of our hands.'

'We'll have to back Tony up,' said Ralph. 'That man might appeal to his "better nature", and I'm afraid he has one.'

'Rot!' said Tony.

'Never mind, Tony,' said Michael. 'With us there, you'll keep it down all right.'

'The food will be filthy,' said Ralph. 'We must organize relays of visitors, and take each other out every Sunday. Then we're sure of one good meal a week.'

'And no giving way to Dudley,' said Michael. 'If he tries to get hold of one of us alone—and he will of each of us in turn—we must say: "I'll have to talk to the others about that," You will be firm, won't you, Tony? You won't give in?'

'No fear!' said Tony.

'He won't enjoy himself as much as he expects,' said Ralph. 'Any admirers he has left will be too low down in the school to matter. What a ghastly place it will be after we're gone—utterly dudleyfied!'

'Well, we shan't be there to see,' said Michael. 'Even Nan and Miss Rigby are going, did you know?'

'Given up hope of Deadly Nightshade?' asked Tony.

'I don't think they like him any more,' said Ralph. 'Nan is pretty sharp with him.'

'Sour grapes, do you think?' said Tony.

'Deadly Nightshade berries,' said Michael. 'She's found out how poisonous they are.'

'And the Rigby has chummed up with her,' said Ralph.

'Yes, it's all lovey dovey between them,' said Michael. 'I expect they'll go to a girls' school, and kiss all the girls goodnight every day, like they do at my sister's school.'

'Then there's the old hag, Knight, Dudley's mother,' said Ralph. 'They wouldn't like her running the place.'

'The swine Girling is listening,' said Michael. 'We said we never spoke against a lady, and he'll sneak if we do.'

'Well, let's give her the benefit of the doubt,' said Ralph. 'We don't know her. She may be a lady, though I should be surprised if she is. Dudley is very common, after all; though he went to a good school.'

'Which is more than the brute Girling is going to do,' said Michael. 'Will they count him as a leaving boy, d'you think?'

'It won't look well in the school mag,' said Ralph. 'After Alan Dearden (Winchester), and Guy Tracy (Rugby) and Daniel Goodbody (Malvern)—to end up with George Girling (Bengers Towers).'

'They'll hush it up,' said Tony.

' "George Girling is also leaving us, to continue his education privately",' said Michael. 'They'll put in something like that.'

'You can't continue what's never been begun,' said Ralph.

'Well, no paper tells the truth,' said Michael. 'Dick will write a piece about Harry (at least I hope Dudley won't do it); but he won't be able to say he was done to death.'

'I hope we shan't be asked to subscribe to a leaving present for the brute Girling,' said Ralph. 'I think we ought to refuse.'

'I wouldn't mind subscribing to have his nose put right,' said Tony. 'It's an eyesore as it is.'

'We shan't see it again,' said Ralph. 'Bengers Towers will keep him out of our world—for life.'

'Dick and Mary will probably give him a book,' said Michael. 'But the school subscribed for a wreath for Harry, his victim: that's our present to him.'

'Dick will probably give him his leaving talk,' said Ralph.

'Well, he'd better know the worst before he goes to Bengers Towers,' said Michael. 'I expect he'll hear Dick's Bible stories with the others.'

'Tell us a Bible story,' said Ralph. 'You're a clergyman's son, Tony.'

'I'll begin,' said Michael. 'The centurion, whose name was Girling, went in unto an harlot and knew her, and she conceived and bore a son ...'

'And she called his name George,' said Tony. 'And his nose was a wonder and a sign to all Israel.'

'There'll be tribes and tribes of Israel at Bengers Towers,' said Ralph.

'My wife and I are leaving Hazelcroft,' said Dick Langton, to the boys assembled for prize-giving. 'I suppose most of you know this already, as your parents have, of course, been told. Mr Knight will carry on, and we wish him every good fortune, and the school with him. My wife and I are probably going to pass our declining years on the Italian Riviera; when we know our address, we shall publish it in the school magazine. We shall be very glad to see all members of the staff and old boys who find themselves near us. They'll be sure of a good cup of tea which, I believe, is rare in those parts. I'm told Italians don't understand about boiling water.'

'The headmaster, with the modesty that we have learned to expect of him, lays down his heavy burden with a few light-hearted words,' said Dudley Knight. 'How great the burden is, I have yet to learn; but with the help of my good mother I hope to shoulder it, and to continue the school we all love in the great tradition of its founders, Mr and Mrs Langton.

'Perhaps my duties may some time give me leisure to take a cup of tea with them in sunny Italy; I will hope so. But at all times Hazelcroft, their old home, will be ready to receive them as honoured and beloved guests— I will say no more, for I find I cannot.'

He gulped, and sat down.

The last prayers of the term followed, and they sang:

> *Let Thy father-hand be shielding*
> *All who here shall meet no more;*
> *May their seed-time past be yielding*
> *Year by year a richer store;*
> *Those returning*
> *Make more faithful than before.*

'I regret the metaphor in the last verse,' said Mary to Kit. 'Because I know your uncle is going to talk to them about their seed.'

'Dudley will tell them all about bees and pollen,' said Kit. 'And how holy and beautiful it all is.'

'They'll get no nonsense of that sort from Dick,' said Mary. 'Oh, dear, I don't like going; and I can't think how Dick will get through the day. After all, a woman has the house to manage.'

'I don't know,' said Kit. 'Sometimes a man can get clear of the past more easily than a woman. Uncle Dick may be able to pull out, and not leave any of his roots behind; that's more than you will do, I'm afraid.'

'Yes, I'm afraid so, Christopher; but now we must forget ourselves and amuse the leaving boys.'

It was a pleasant occasion, and the boys (a little afraid of their coming experience) played up with nervous courage.

Anita and Nan disappeared together; Dudley stalked off alone, for no one desired his company. Mary and Kit walked on the terrace.

'"The usher walks alone, A melancholy man,"' quoted Kit.

'Dick is somewhere down there,' said Mary, with a vague gesture. 'Telling the boys racy Old Testament stories.'

'"Those grand old stories", Dudley would call them,' said Kit. 'I'm sure they lose nothing in Uncle Dick's telling of them.'

'She was a whore; boys will pronounce it *hwore*, when they're reading the Bible,' they heard Dick saying.

'I know they do,' said Kit. 'They've been calling George Girling's mother that, to annoy him. Matron wanted to stop it, but I persuaded her that it wasn't worth the bother.'

'Sweet innocents!' said Mary. 'How could she succeed in that not uncrowded profession with a face like hers?'

'And I suppose she would have had to learn how to please,' said Kit. 'She's very unpleasing.'

'They're coming this way again,' said Mary. 'Dick seems to like that bit of lawn; I hope they can't see us.'

'Ought we to move?'

185

'Don't let's bother,' said Mary.

'Now, Onan, you remember about him,' said Dick.

'It really is an Old Testament lesson,' murmured Kit.

'Dogs are very fond of it,' said the headmaster. 'You must have noticed our dogs? It's the worst possible thing for your training; you're all keen on games, so I'm sure you'll keep off it.'

'I suppose that's what games are for,' murmured Kit.

'Like Matrimony, for those "who have not the gift of continence",' said Mary.

'You mean, you marry when you give up games?' said Kit. 'And go straight from one bondage to another? Sad.'

Dick drew near again, he was talking about Lot. 'They didn't want his daughters,' he said. 'They wanted the men.'

'Funny thing, Sodomy,' he went on. 'Never appealed to me—but you'll find it rife in the public schools. Two boys were expelled from Ragstead for it last year, and four from Slowborough. There were some cases of it at Bengers Towers too; one of the partners had to go abroad. It's against the law, you see. However, if you're sensible, and only make friends with boys of your own age...'

'He must have put them through the lot by now,' said Kit.

'Oh, I think there's a little more,' said Mary. 'They're told that betting is "a mug's game", and they're advised not to start smoking till they've stopped growing.'

'I suppose we've missed most of it, any way.'

'Yes, all the part about nasty diseases,' said Mary. 'But that's rather gruesome; I'm glad we escaped it.'

'Goodnight, boys.'

'Goodnight, sir; thank you, sir.'

The leaving boys made their way up the path, and greeted Kit and Mary.

'Dick didn't exactly tell us how to do any of these things,' they heard a regretful voice saying.

'Never mind,' said Mary softly. 'They'll find out.'